44 Tiny Chefs

Sylvia Bishop

Illustrated by Ashley King

LITTLE TIGER

LONDON

For my excellent sisters, Jenny and Flo x
~ SB

For Richard,
with the warmest of ginger hearts x
~ AK

CHAPTER ONE

THE TROUBLE WITH CAKES

It was the first day of the spring holidays, and Betsy Bow-Linnet was locked in a deadly battle with a chocolate éclair.

The éclair had to be eaten. Her father Bertram had made it, and he was hovering next to her armchair in the parlour, looking hopeful and excited.

But Betsy had already eaten profiteroles and raspberry turnovers and choux buns and custard tarts and cream meringues and doughnuts and a lot of things that didn't even have names – but they all had plenty of sugar and cream. Everything had been delicious, but she had stopped enjoying herself about ten cakes ago. About eight cakes ago, her mother Bella had suddenly remembered some urgent piano practice she had to do. About five cakes ago, Grandad had suddenly remembered a nap he was meant to have. He was having it now, snoring loudly in his armchair to show how definitely asleep he was.

"I think it's the closest I've got, B," said Bertram. "The trick was to double the cream."

"Oh," said Betsy faintly. "Right."

She picked up the éclair. One point to Betsy.

The éclair oozed a slug of cream, and glistened menacingly. She hesitated. One point to the éclair.

From inside the piano her mice squeaked encouragement. Betsy had forty-four highly trained African pygmy mice, and they were very clever at a lot of things, including playing the piano. But they couldn't eat chocolate without being *very* ill, so there was no way they could help her now.

Betsy took a deep breath.

Then the phone rang, and Bertram went to get it. From the quiver in his voice, Betsy suspected it was his terrifying Great-Aunt Agatha, calling to remind him that he was due at hers for dinner tonight – as though he would ever forget. She quickly shoved the éclair in among an especially frondy fern. She would have to remember to get it later.

She felt horrible about tricking him, and

the horribleness ballooned when Bertram came back in and smiled at her empty plate. "Tasty?"

"Mmm. Delicious."

He beamed. "There are plenty more in the fridge."

This was enormously true. The fridge was full to bursting. Bertram had stuck a sign on the door saying HELP YOURSELF TO CAKES!, but then he had smeared some melted chocolate across the middle, so now it just said HELP (splodge) CAKES! Which was about right.

Betsy wasn't sure how to reply, but luckily Bertram was already wondering out loud whether the extra-cream trick would work with apple turnovers, and then he was off to the kitchen to try it. As soon as he had gone, Grandad woke up suspiciously quickly from his nap and gave Betsy a Look.

"So," he said. "Where did you put it, B?"

There was no point lying to Grandad. "In the ferns. Grandad, has … has Dad gone mad?"

Grandad wagged his elbows thoughtfully, setting off a Mexican wave of bobbing and bowing among the ferns, then said, "What makes you think he wasn't mad to start with?"

This was a fair point.

"Your dad," Grandad went on, "needs something to do. He's needed something to do ever since he gave up the piano, and it's been driving him quietly mad for a while. Now he's found it. This is the sanest he's been for a long time – he's just got a bit overexcited, that's all."

Betsy thought about this. It made sense. Bertram used to be a pianist like Bella. But secretly he had been using his own pygmy mice to play for him – just like Betsy's mice, there were forty-four, one for every two notes of the piano. Last summer he had come clean to Bella and the family about it, and once everything was out in the open, he had given the whole thing up. Now he mostly just did crosswords, and ate cream cakes. It was nearly his birthday, and for weeks he had been planning the massive cream cake he would order for the occasion. When the bakery down the road had shut down and the best cream cakes in town were no more, he had gone to bed for two whole days.

Then he had started baking.

He was, it turned out, exceptionally good at it. And it really made him happy – in fact, he was the happiest Betsy had ever seen him. But the happiness depended on people wanting to eat his cakes.

"I don't think I can eat any more," said Betsy now. "We're going to have to stop pretending at some point, aren't we?"

"Oh, I don't know," said Grandad. "You could just keep feeding the ferns."

"Grandad, there are loads of ferns, but there aren't *infinity* ferns. And I think there might be infinity cakes." And for a moment there was silence, as they both contemplated this fate.

Grandad recovered from the thought first.

"I was only joking, B. You're right, of course. We just have to say it gently."

"Maybe we should start hinting now," said Betsy. "We can sort of lead up to it."

"Excellent idea, B," said Grandad. He said it in the special way that means, *It is an excellent idea, which* you *should carry out, because I am very comfy in this armchair.* He looked as though another nap might come on very fast. So Betsy stood up, put a couple of mice in the curls of her hair for moral support, and headed for the kitchen.

The kitchen was filled with a soft, sweet smell. Even though she was sick of cakes, Betsy thought the smell was wonderful. The mice agreed. Their noses trembled in awe.

In the middle of all the lovely smell stood Bertram, looking sadly at the fridge. He took some cakes out. He replaced them with other cakes. He shook his head.

Betsy coughed. "Dad?"

"Oh, hello, B."

"You OK?"

"Yes, yes." There was a pause. "The fridge," he said, "is full." He considered this. "Do you think," he asked, "I've made too many cakes?"

"Oh, no!" lied Betsy. He looked so forlorn that she abandoned her hinting mission without a second thought.

"But," said Bertram, "no one has been eating them. And now the fridge is full."

This was a very sensible argument. The blob of cream on the end of his nose was less sensible. But overall, he had a point.

"I'm just saving mine," Betsy heard herself say, "because I want to have them for dinner."

Bertram perked up with such

speed that the blob of cream on his nose

wibbled right off. "Really?"

"Really," said Betsy, while what she thought

was, *oh help.*

Still, her father was happy again. And tonight he would be out for his monthly dinner with his terrifying Great-Aunt Agatha, so she would have a chance to get rid of a box or two, somehow. She would start the letting-him-down-gently plan tomorrow. Almost certainly.

Bertram hated visiting terrifying Great-Aunt Agatha. Betsy didn't blame him. She had only met her great-aunt twice, and she had no wish ever to repeat the experience. But when the hour approached, Bertram took off his apron with brave determination, and left the sweet-smelling kitchen with the air of a soldier leaving for battle.

As soon as he had gone, Bella's urgent piano practice was abruptly over; Grandad found a sudden burst of energy and got up from his armchair at last, and even the mice seemed relieved. Betsy brought their tank to the kitchen and fed them their evening pumpkin seeds. The humans weren't hungry at all, but Bella said they had to eat *something* that wasn't ninety-five per cent cream, so they each had a token supper of three lettuce leaves and a bean.

While they ate, Betsy told the others about her promise to eat cakes for dinner, and they all had a think about where to hide some. Bertram was sure to see them if they were just thrown in the bin.

It was Bella who suggested taking some to the neighbours. "They might like a few each," she said. "After all, they *are* very good, in normal quantities." This was true. In fact, they were superb. And giving them away felt much better than throwing them away.

"There's some greaseproof paper here

somewhere," Bella went on, getting up from the table. The contents of the kitchen had all been spilled out on to the surfaces in the baking frenzy. She began the search through recipe books and piping bags and spatulas and rolling pins, provoking plumes of flour. "We can wrap the cakes in that. If I can ever find it... Let's see, who do we know in the road? There's the Fortesques and the Khatris and the Macavoys..."

"And the Joneses," said Betsy, "and the Angelis..." And she helped her mother hunt down the greaseproof paper and recall neighbours, while Grandad quietly fed his unwanted bean to a mouse. Paper located, they wrapped up oozing parcels of cakes, Bella showing Betsy how to seal them with a smart twist of the paper. Then Betsy took them to the neighbours.

Everyone was delighted. They thanked Betsy over and over again, and smiled the free, happy smiles of people who have never had to eat more than ten cream cakes in one day. So *that* was all right. In fact, it was almost nice. Betsy didn't feel too guilty about it, and when she went to bed that night, she drifted straight into untroubled sleep.

The next morning Betsy woke early, but

when she came downstairs Bertram was already in the kitchen, waiting for something in the oven to rise. He was looking wistfully at a copy of the *London Natter*. This was odd. Normal expressions when reading the *London Natter* are bored, very bored, painfully bored, or asleep.

"Morning, Dad. What are you reading about?"

He turned the *Natter* to show her. It was a full-page colour advert for something called the MEGA-MIX-O-MATIC, which was apparently *A MUST-HAVE item for EVERY BAKER*. There was a photo, and it looked like a whole kitchen had been in a tragic accident. Spoons, whisks, knives, forks and other less-identifiable objects stuck out at all angles from a shiny silver cube.

"It looks wonderful," said Bertram. "But it's a bit of a silly price."

Betsy had five pounds to spend on Bertram's birthday, which was in four days. Since he wasn't getting a giant cream cake any more, maybe he could have a Mega-mix-o-matic.

She looked at the number below the picture. It was quite a lot more than five pounds.

"So," said Bertram, "that's enough of *that*. Back to the baking. I see from the fridge that a certain someone had cakes for dinner… What do you fancy today, B?"

This was it: time for operation letting-Dad-down-gently. Betsy took a deep breath, which smelled of cake-and-warmth-and-joy-and-homeliness, and said, "Dad—"

And then the doorbell rang.

"I'll get it!" she said, grateful for the distraction.

It was Mrs Fortesque, who lived one door to the right. Betsy hastily stepped outside and pulled the door to, so that Bertram wouldn't hear anything he shouldn't. What was Mrs Fortesque doing here so early?

The two families got on OK-ish. Once, admittedly, there had been an argument. A-to-A-sharp third octave had escaped and ended up in the Fortesques' house, and Mrs Fortesque had tried to hoover him up, while Mr Fortesque stood on a table screaming. A-to-A-sharp had chewed through the wire on the hoover. The Bow-Linnets thought this was a very reasonable response to being chased with a hoover; the Fortesques disagreed.

Anyway, now Mrs Fortesque was smiling brightly at Betsy, like a woman who has never in her life sent angry invoices for a new hoover, or threatened to call the police and the council and the fire brigade.

"Betsy!" she said. "Just the girl I wanted to see. I'm having a little party this afternoon, and I wondered if you had any more of those *delicious* home-made cream cakes."

"Um," said Betsy, hesitating. The answer was YES, of course. She was just wondering how to avoid awkward questions from Bertram about how, exactly, Mrs Fortesque had come to know about his cakes.

Mrs Fortesque misread the hesitation. "*Please*," she said. "Everybody would *love* them. I'd be happy to pay you for them."

And that was when Betsy had a glorious idea.

"All right," she agreed. "One pound a cake. Come back in an hour and I'll have a parcel for you."

Mrs Fortesque beamed, and promised she would be there in one hour precisely. Betsy let herself back inside, her head rushing with the brilliance of her plan – which was this:

She would sell Bertram's cakes. She wouldn't tell him until his birthday, when she would give him two surprises at once. The first would be to tell him that his cakes were so popular the town had been queueing up to buy them. And the second would be the Mega-mix-o-matic, which she would buy with the cake money.

She hurried to find Grandad and Bella, who

were in the parlour.

"I've got an idea," Betsy whispered. "For Dad's birthday. Do we have more greaseproof paper for wrapping cakes?"

Grandad looked at her over his paper. "Betsy Bow-Linnet, you cannot give your father his *own cakes* for his birthday."

"No," said Betsy, "that's not what I mean." And she whispered her plan to them, tumbling through it all the way up to "*And* it means we won't have to eat all the cream cakes he makes", before finally pausing for breath.

"Brilliant, B!" said Grandad, with an enthusiastic pump of his elbows.

"Marvellous, darling," said Bella. "Let's start at once!"

So they did. Grandad got a fold-up table from the shed, Bella went down the road to the corner shop to buy more greaseproof paper, some ribbon and a birthday card, and Betsy casually piled a platter of cream cakes in the kitchen, trying to look as though she was just a bit peckish. Bertram beamed, apparently thinking this an entirely reasonable amount of cake. Then Betsy took four of the most sensible of the mice, and went with Grandad to set up the table at the end of the road. Bella stayed at home to keep watch on Bertram, and to give Mrs Fortesque her cakes.

They laid out their shop under a blossom tree, which cast a pool of shade, and smelled so sweet that even the cakes were outdone.

Betsy wrote out a sign: FRESH CREAM CAKES – £1 EACH! Grandad tore the greaseproof paper into sheets to wrap the cakes in, and wrote THE BOW-LINNET BAKERY on each one. Betsy showed the mice how to tie up the parcels of cake with the ribbon. Then she put out the birthday card for people to sign.

Within minutes they had their first customers. And as word spread, a queue started to form, and it got longer and longer and longer. Bella had to keep bringing them more cakes, telling Bertram sort of honestly that some of them were for her friends, but taking care not to give away the whole plan.

They were an efficient team. Grandad wrapped the cakes and the mice tied them up with ribbon, while Betsy took people's orders, put the money in her big change jar, and asked if they would like to sign Bertram's card. The jar of change grew heavier, and the card filled up with birthday wishes and drooling praise for the cakes.

THE
BOW-LINNE
BAKERY

FRESH
CREAM CAKES
-£1 EACH!

They stayed out until it was too dark to see the change, and then stayed a minute longer anyway because there was still a queue; until at last a sudden spring shower forced them to pack away. But by that time Betsy already had enough money for the Mega-mix-o-matic *and* a birthday balloon.

As they hurried home, it was hard to mind the rain. They were too giddy with their success. Betsy didn't think *anything* could ruin that day.

This was incorrect.

Grandad snuck around the back to put the table in the shed, and Betsy let herself in by the front door. Bella was there in the hall, looking pale, hands fidgeting.

"Hi, we came home 'cause it's raining, but it went *really* well," said Betsy – then she looked properly at her mother and said, "What is it?"

"She's in the living room with Dad," said Bella. "She says she wants to see all of us, I don't know why, she won't say, she's just been sitting there waiting... I tried to give her excuses, Betsy, but she just rapped me on the knees with her walking stick and carried on sitting there."

"Who?" said Betsy. "Is it...?" But she already knew the answer. There was only one person whose walking stick was also used for knee-rapping.

Bella nodded. "Yes. Great-Aunt Agatha."

CHAPTER TWO

THE HALF-MOON BAKERY

The parlour was filled with a magnificent silence, apart from the pattering of the rain against the windows. It seemed to Betsy that the ferns had curled inwards sadly, which might have just been because the sunlight was gone. But then again, Bertram and Bella had curled inwards too, and *they* weren't plants.

Great-Aunt Agatha sat in Betsy's favourite armchair, and Great-Aunt Agatha's walking stick sat in Grandad's. Betsy went to sit on the

piano stool, and looked from Bertram to Bella
to the tower of her terrifying great-aunt. She
was swathed in heavy black knitwear, with a
heavily knitted brow to match, all topped off
with a mad nest of iron-grey hair. In Betsy's
own hair, four soggy mice shivered.

"So," said Great-Aunt
Agatha. When she
spoke, it was like
a gong being
struck. "You have
been selling
cakes."

Bertram, who was used to agreeing with his great-aunt, said, "Yes, yes, absolutely." Then his brain caught up with the situation, and he said, "Have we?"

Great-Aunt Agatha's lungs heaved as she prepared to speak again, so Betsy had to get in fast. "Me and Grandad have, Dad. It was going to be a surprise. Everyone loves your cakes, and they've all signed a birthday card for you saying how great they are, and we were going to use the money to buy you a Mega-mix-o-matic. We've already got enough *and* enough for a balloon because your cakes are brilliant."

She paused to breathe in, and watched her father. His face went through every shade of pink, and his eyes widened and widened, and he opened and shut his mouth.

"Gosh," he said at last. And it was a pleased

sort of gosh. *Very* pleased.

Great-Aunt Agatha, however, was not pleased. "Gosh," she intoned, "is not the word I would use, Bertram. Your child has been selling cakes from a street-corner stall, like an uncouth ragamuffin."

"Agatha, really—" Bella began, but then Great-Aunt Agatha gave her a Look which was fifty gongs at once, and Bella suddenly took an enormous interest in the nearest fern and didn't finish her sentence.

Agatha produced a sheet of *Bow-Linnet's Bakery* greaseproof paper from her bag. She glowered at the offending object, then at each Bow-Linnet in turn. "Mrs Pipsworth brought this to my lady's coffee morning today, along with tattling tales about your baking exploits, Bertram. My family's name, scrawled on a piece of rubbish. I," she clarified, "am ashamed."

"Now look here, Great-Aunt," said Bertram. His face had picked a shade of pink to settle on, and he pushed his glasses up his nose with all the vim of a man who has just discovered that he is an Admired Chef. "You can't just come into my house and start—"

"And as for you, Bertram –" Great-Aunt Agatha rolled on, because she *could* just come into his house and start, and what's more, she could middle and end too – "I am extraordinarily disappointed in you. Those cream cakes Mrs Pipsworth brought me were absolutely superb. What have you been playing at, man, squandering that talent? Sitting around playing the piano all these years like a nincompoop!"

Bella bristled. Great-Aunt Agatha had never approved of the family's music. She preferred something solid – something you could hold, and preferably rap with a walking stick.

Bella was ready to defend pianos. Betsy wanted to defend Bertram. Bertram was still trying to defend Betsy. All three Bow-Linnets opened their mouths.

"I have bought you a bakery," said Great-Aunt Agatha.

All three Bow-Linnets shut their mouths and looked at each other.

"What?" said Bertram – and, "*When?*" said Bella.

Great-Aunt Agatha ignored Bertram, deeming *what* an unworthy question, and turned instead to Bella. "This afternoon.

I went to the estate agent in person. He made a ridiculous fuss about everything, but I didn't leave until he had finished all his piffling paperwork and phone calls and given me the keys." She said this with enormous satisfaction. Betsy strongly suspected the walking stick had been involved.

"You –" the old woman went on, raising a finger to point at Betsy – "will stop hawking wares on street corners like a common urchin. You –" she swivelled the finger to Bertram – "will stop lazing around when you have a perfectly good talent. And you –" she said to Grandad, who had just come in from putting the table away – "are soggy."

Grandad shrugged, elbows flapping water on to the floor. "It's raining."

"Then why did you go outside?"

"It's good for the soul, Agatha," he replied. "You should try it. What's going on?"

"Your family can explain," said Agatha. "I have said all I came here to say. The key and papers are in the envelope on the table, Bertram. And do think of another name. The Bow-Linnet Bakery is twee." And with that, she took her stick, swept up to her full height, and marched to the door. On her way, she rapped Grandad's elbow neatly into place against his side with the stick.

"Goodbye," she said. And she left the room without looking back.

"Thank you?" said Bertram, as she shut the door. And he looked at the others, who shrugged. It didn't *feel* like a thank you sort of situation. But then there was the brown envelope waiting on the table.

Betsy picked it up, passed it to Bertram, and curled up in her chair, making her own familiar dents in the seat to get rid of Great-Aunt Agatha's. Now that her great-aunt was gone, four mice ventured their noses cautiously over the top of her hair, and the other forty over the top of their tank. "Open it, Dad," she said.

Bertram opened it. He pulled out the contents. There was a wad of papers, and a single brass key.

DEEDS

12 Hawthorne Street

"Title deeds," Bertram read aloud, "for 12 Hawthorne Street."

"But that's Angelo's!" said Betsy. Angelo's was Bertram's favourite bakery – the one that had closed down and sent him to bed for two days, before his baking frenzy.

"Did she…?" Grandad guessed. "So do we…?" The others confirmed that she had and they did. Grandad looked astonished, and just a *little* admiring. "That woman," he said, "could move a mountain in one minute flat if it was in her way."

There was a pause; no one could think of anything big enough to say. Bertram was gazing at his key, dumbfounded. At last he cleared his throat, and said, "Thank you, B."

"It was Great-Aunt Agatha, not me. And it was *your* cakes that made her do it."

"Ah, but if you hadn't sold my cakes…"
Bertram was all pink again. "That's the kind of idea I would never, ever have had, B. You're full of all these Big Ideas. It amazes me. And now, thanks to you, we have our very own bakery." He got up to hug her, being careful not to squash the mice, and said, "I'm still very cross that she called you an uncouth ragamuffin."

"It's all right," said Betsy. "I don't really know what that means." And it really was all right, because she was glowing from what Bertram had said. It had never occurred to her that her ideas might be bigger than average. But she *did* have a habit of making unusual things happen.

"What are we standing around for?" said Grandad. "Let's go and see your bakery!"

So they set out. The rain had stopped and there was a creamy half-moon in the sky, which was perfect: Bella always said that half-moon nights were Bertram's lucky nights, on account of his half-moon glasses. They all looked up at the half-moon, and made wishes.

It wasn't a long walk, and they were there at Angelo's in no time. Betsy hadn't seen it since it had closed. It looked … different. The bright sign saying *Angelo's* had been taken down, the shelves had been taken out of the window, and the whole place was dark and silent.

Bertram turned the key in the lock, and opened the door. The bell over the door didn't tinkle, because it wasn't there any more.

Bella tried the light, but it wasn't working.

They crowded in silently. All of the fizz inside Betsy had fallen flat. She had been imagining the old warmly lit bakery with its sweet smells and its clutter of tables and chairs.

This dark place only smelled of dust, and by the light of a streetlight outside, they could see that the room was empty.

They didn't own a bakery. Not yet. They owned an empty room, and an enormous challenge.

But while Betsy and Bella and Grandad stood uncertainly in the middle of the room, and the four mice peered out from Betsy's hair like explorers from a ship, Bertram strode to the door at the back and pulled it open. He turned on the light in the room behind – which worked.

His eyes widened in wonder. "*Oh,*" he said.

The others crowded in. "*Oh,*" they all agreed.

It was the kitchen. Silver gleamed from all sides. Towers of silvery ovens; stacks of silvery trays for dough to prove on and freshly baked cakes to cool; a silvery worktop for shaping and kneading and rolling out the dough; silvery fridges, for buckets of cream and piles of cream cakes.

Bertram squeezed Betsy's hand. "Look at it, B," he said. "Look what your Big Ideas have done."

"It was Great-Aunt Agatha mostly," said Betsy fairly. Then, remembering her great-aunt's instructions, she had a thought: "What are you going to call it, Dad?"

Bertram looked around at all the shining silver, and out through the window, at the cream-cake moon. "How about the Half-Moon Bakery?" he said. "For good luck."

And everybody agreed that this was just right. It *was* a good name.

And they were going to need the luck.

CHAPTER THREE

THE BAKING BEGINS

Bertram wanted to have an opening party for the bakery on his birthday.

"But that's in three days, Bertie," said Bella. And he just nodded, and pushed his spectacles more firmly up his nose. Every now and then, you could glimpse traces of Great-Aunt Agatha in Betsy's father.

Bella knew him well enough to know when his mind was made up. "All right, then," she said. "We'd better get started. There's a lot to do."

And she was right. They began that night by drawing up a guest list, which was no small task; there were so many friends to invite, not to mention all the people-who-are-not-really-friends-but-we-probably-ought-to-invite-them-or-they'll-be-offended, like the Fortesques, and the dreaded Vera Brick.

Bertram stayed up writing out invitations, and Betsy volunteered to post them first thing next morning. And, because she had Big Ideas and made things happen, she added a few invitations of her own: to the *London Natter*, and to fancy pastry chefs all over the country, and the owners of important shops like Harrods, and even the Royal Taster of Fine Foods for Her Majesty

TO HARRODS

PURNELL'S

TO THE LONDON NATTER

TO ROYAL TASTER OF FINE FOODS FOR HER MAJESTY THE QUEEN

the Queen. She didn't tell anyone – not even Grandad. She whispered it to the mice, of course, but they didn't count.

Then there was a day of shopping. Bella had to teach, but the rest of them spent the whole day traipsing from shop to shop. The kitchen needed all kinds of pans and bowls and knives and spoons and whisks and whatnottery, not to mention sacks of flour and sugar and jugs of cream and huge glass jars filled with raisins and chocolate drops and glacé cherries and sprinkles and almond flakes and silver balls. And of course, Betsy took her jar of change and bought a sparkling Mega-mix-o-matic, which took pride of place on the counter.

And that wasn't all. The shop itself needed glass-fronted shelves for the cakes, and tables and spindly chairs and thick lemon-yellow

tablecloths and a new lightbulb. It was a
long day.

The next day everything had to be put in
place in the shop, and someone came to paint
THE HALF-MOON BAKERY in swirling
gold over the door. Betsy stayed at home with
the mice, because they were getting restless
– and they were *not* permitted in the bakery.
Besides, the invitations had all been received
now, and people were ringing the house to say
they would be coming. Betsy was desperate
to know if anyone she had invited would
call.

She let the mice out of their tank, but they
didn't want to play the piano or practise
acrobatics or any of their usual tricks. They
were distracted, and sniffed enviously at
everyone who popped home from the bakery

for something, and kept scuttling off to nose at the bags and boxes that were still in the hall. They knew when they were being left out of things.

"Nope. That's all special," Betsy said, stopping one runaway from crawling inside a box, and holding him up in her palm. "Sorry. How about you play in the kitchen here? Dad's not using it any more. I'm sure it's fine for you to be there."

Actually, she wasn't *entirely* sure, so she started by training them to be extra well behaved. She trailed pumpkin seeds into a little bowl of water to encourage them all to wash their paws, and whenever they nibbled something they shouldn't she ate a pumpkin seed herself, which was their special signal for *no* – although they didn't need warning away

46

from anything that would be really poisonous for them, like chocolate. They seemed to know by instinct. They *loved* the kitchen, leaving little paw-print patterns in the flour and jumping up and down on the springy scales and trying out the piping bags, which they were surprisingly good at.

At last the bakery was ready, and it was the day of the party itself: they had cakes to make. The Mega-mix-o-matic was working at full speed, and every Bow-Linnet was pitching in to help Bertram. Grandad, with his excellent elbow power, turned out to be a very good whisker. Bella, with her gentle pianist's touch, could shape dough into impossibly delicate shapes, and her fingers were moving in a furious flurry all day.

Betsy was an enthusiastic baker, but had a habit of making everything come out gloopy or lumpy or shrivelled or something else it wasn't supposed to be. It was very disheartening.

"Why don't you try piping the icing and cream for the finished cakes?" suggested Bella, when they were back home for lunch. "Do you think she could try, Bertie? We haven't even started on that yet."

"What? Mm. Yes," said Bertram, who was having difficulty concentrating on anything that wasn't baking. He had hardly eaten any of his food, and instead was absent-mindedly shaping it into little cake-piles on his plate.

So that afternoon, Betsy sat in the front of the shop with a tray of cakes and a set of piping bags, and when Bertram saw the beautiful results he assigned her to do all the rest of the piping. As soon as he had gone back into the kitchen, Grandad raised his eyebrows at the so-delicate icing, then at Betsy.

"All right," he whispered, "where are the mice?"

"Up my sleeve," said Betsy, letting half a dozen mice scurry back out. "I know Dad didn't want me to, but I trained them to use piping bags yesterday and they're *so* good, and they're really well behaved about washing their paws and not nibbling anything, I promise.

Three of them put pressure on the bag
while the other three guide the nozzle –
look…"

"Clever devils," said Grandad. "Just don't let
your father see them. He might combust."

There was no danger of Bertram noticing
anything. He was whirling about even faster
than the Mega-mix-o-matic. With an hour
to go they finally stopped, exhausted, and
covered from head-to-toe in flour – even
Betsy, who hadn't been in the kitchen.
Bella had to put ice packs on her fingers,
which were painfully stiff from making the
same movements over and over again, and
Grandad's elbows were black and blue. But
they were victorious.

Every counter in the kitchen was crammed
with a resplendent array of cakes.

Cream cakes, of course, were the speciality. But there were also sponge cakes and pastries and brownies and muffins and tartlets and shortbread and macaroons. Arguably, they had overdone it. But it looked magnificent.

"Right," said Grandad, "I don't know much about parties, but I *think* it isn't normal to be

wearing this much flour."

"I'm not sure how I've done this," said Bella, "but there's dough between my toes."

"Let's go and change," said Betsy. She was very aware of the wriggling mice in her sleeve, and she needed to get them home; she couldn't risk a guest seeing them, and getting all upset about mice in a bakery.

They hurried home, leaving a floury trail, and Betsy raced upstairs to her room. She put the six mice away, and counted out pumpkin-seed rewards. "Well done," she said. "You were brilliant. Sorry you can't come to the party."

The mice cleaned their whiskers, as if to say that they weren't interested in a silly party anyway, and curled up for a well-earned rest.

Next Betsy raced to the answering machine, and her heart leaped, because there were *loads* of messages. But although they were all from people calling to say they would come, none of them were the important people Betsy had invited. She listened to every single one – including, unfortunately, one from Vera Brick – until there was a click, and the machine said: "No more messages."

For a moment she stood staring at it, as though it might say, "Oh wait, I forgot one." It didn't. So she pulled herself together, went upstairs, washed off the flour, and put on her green dress which swirled when she walked, and her shoes which went clickety-click. Clickety-clicking her heels for luck, she felt hopeful again. They might just come without calling first. Lots of people probably would. It was that sort of party.

And just as she was thinking this, the telephone rang.

She jumped up and ran to the door – but there was her dad with a flower in his hand, just about to knock. Betsy heard Bella picking up the telephone downstairs, and she had to make a very big effort to look pleased about the flower. It was an old tradition of her dad's, and it *was* nice of him, but it was also very annoying right now.

"Ah! Hello, B," said Bertram. He held up the flower, and she saw his hand was shaking slightly with nervous excitement. "I was wondering," he said, "if Betsy Bow-Linnet would do me the honour of wearing this flower in her hair tonight?"

Betsy thanked him, and let him put the flower in her hair, which was a bit fiddly on account of the nervous-excitement-shaking. Then, as he was still saying, "Beautiful, B!" she yelled, "Thanks, Dad!" and raced down the stairs two at a time.

Bella had almost finished. But Betsy was just in time to find her looking pleased and pink and a bit flustered, and saying, "Yes, of course. Don't worry at all about the short notice. It's an honour."

Mimblemimble, said the phone.

"Well, I hope you'll enjoy it."

Mimble.

"Yes, see you for the party! Thank you."

Betsy was practically hopping up and down. When Bella had hung up, she squealed, "Who was—?" – but then there was her father again, looking a bit helplessly at a tie he had done up all wrong; and as Bella corrected it for him, she murmured to Betsy, "Best if I tell you later, darling. Let's just get ready now."

Betsy saw her point: Bertram didn't need to be made any more nervous. She was desperate to know, but she kept quiet.

When Bertram's tie was on the right way, and Grandad had successfully persuaded Bella that he wasn't going to wear a tie and that there was nothing at all wrong with his old jumper, they hurried to the bakery. Suddenly, Bertram wasn't the only one who was nervous. For a minute, they waited on their new spindly chairs in silence.

Then the door opened, and the first guest arrived.

CHAPTER FOUR

An Important Guest

Once the arrivals began, there was barely time to offer one guest a cake before the next guest turned up. They grew to a gaggle, which grew to a throng, which grew to a group-that-is-too-large-to-reasonably-fit-inside-a-small-bakery. Bertram moved the lemon-tables and their chairs outside, and the party spilled out on to the street.

Great-Aunt Agatha didn't come – she had been invited, by post *and* telephone, but had only replied, "Good heavens, *no* thank you," and hung up the phone. Betsy moved between the people with a tray of cakes. She had no idea who most of the people there were, so it was hard to guess who Bella's mystery caller might be. But there were *some* people she knew. A hugely bearded man and a muscular woman were friends of hers from the circus, and there were people that she knew from Bella's parties. They were mostly nice, except...

"Vera Brick incoming," hissed Grandad, appearing out of the crowd at Betsy's elbow. "On your left, with your father. Quick, look busy." And he started rearranging cakes, with a puzzled frown, as though it was *very* difficult and *very* important.

Betsy reached for a profiterole with the same earnest gravity, but she was too slow.

"My, my," said Vera to Bertram (she never spoke to Betsy directly), "what a busy little helper you have. I hear she started the whole affair, Bertram, selling cakes in the street!" And she laughed her honking laugh, even though nothing was funny. Except maybe her hat, which was huge and puffy and ridiculous.

"Yes, Betsy was brilliant," said Bertram loyally, leaning back to avoid being clouted by the hat.

"It's a good thing my Vernon didn't come to inspect *that* little cake shop! I doubt it would have passed!" She honked some more, and the man next to her nodded gravely. Betsy didn't know him. "Perhaps," said Vera, addressing a shelf just over Betsy's left shoulder, "Betsy hasn't met my husband? Vernon is the Chief Health and Safety Inspector for the Greater London Area. He will need to pay this lovely café a little visit, of course." And this she followed up with yet more honking, until she choked on a crumb of custard tart, and had to be slapped on the back by the Chief Health and Safety Inspector Mr Vernon Brick.

When he had finished the slapping, he extended a hand to Betsy. He stared at her intensely, with bulging eyes.

"We shall meet again," he said solemnly. "It will be my duty to inspect this new bakery. I have the right to inspect it at any time of day or night – any time at all. And it shall be a surprise visit, to rule out any hoodwinkery." On this last word, his eyes bulged more than ever.

"Oh," said Betsy. "Well, I promise we don't have any of that. Would you like a yum-yum?" And she picked up the plate.

"I do not," explained Vernon, "eat cakes."

Betsy nearly told him that he was very much at the wrong party, but she managed to stop herself just in time. She returned the plate to its place – then noticed with horror the tiny paw print in the icing of one of the uppermost yum-yums. Had Vernon seen it?

His bulging eyes stared at the yum-yum, but then, they stared at everything. Betsy picked it up and crammed it in her mouth. There was an awkward little silence.

"Well, well," said Bertram, "we'll look forward to it, Vernon. And maybe we can tempt you to a cake when you inspect us – just to do the job thoroughly!"

This was a joke, but Vernon explained,

at some length, why this was not how you inspected a cake shop. Betsy did lots of polite nodding while she chewed, and Bertram said "I see" at helpful intervals. Under her hat, Vera began nodding off.

"Oh," she said, when Vernon started explaining the Post-Inspection Procedure, "is that Emilia Oggely-Fipps? Do excuse me. I *must* say hello." And she was off, hat aloft.

Betsy was a bit worried she would be stuck with Vernon all night. Happily, when Vera's hat moved aside, Vernon spotted Betsy's circus friends. His eyes bulged in alarm. "What an unsafe beard!" he said. "Why, it's a trip hazard and a fire hazard at the same time. I must inform that fellow immediately."

"Good idea," said Betsy, who more than trusted the man in question to handle Vernon

Brick and his beard inspection. She looked around at the other guests, studying their faces for a clue. Was the myster caller here yet?

Grandad, who had been rearranging cakes so thoroughly that even Betsy had forgotten he was there, watched her with narrowed eyes. He could always tell when she was up to something. "B," he said. "What—"

But before he could finish the question, a man appeared at Bertram's side and *ahrrm*ed politely. Betsy, Bertram and Grandad all stopped to look at him. He was the sort of person you looked at. He had a bright blue silk suit, with enormous lacy shirt cuffs poking out at the ends.

"May I interrupt and intervene, Mr Bow-Linnet?" he asked.

Bertram nodded.

"Mr Bow-Linnet," said the man, "My name is Alexander Papparell. I am the Royal Taster of Fine Foods for Her Majesty the Queen."

Bertram's face turned big and round with surprise. Betsy's heart skipped a beat.

This was it!

Alexander Papparell adjusted the enormous lacy cuffs of his shirt and nodded graciously, as though he was taking a tiny bow. "Sir," he said, "it is with pleasure, sincerity and reverence –" with each word he twirled a hand, and his lace cuffs whirled – "that I must share with you the wonder that I have felt tonight. These cakes are exquisite." (More twirling.) "Extraordinary." (A double twirl.) "Electrifying." (An elaborate figure of eight.) "Mr Bow-Linnet, a Royal Gala is being arranged at short notice for this Sunday, and I am tasked with organizing the refreshments. And I would like to ask you to provide cakes for Her Majesty and her guests."

Bertram was speechless. It took all Betsy's self-control not to hop up and down. Her Big Idea had worked!

After a slight pause while Bertram got over his speechlessness, he thanked Alexander Papparell, and shook his hand, and agreed.

"Splendid!" said Alexander. "Delightful! I will come tomorrow to discuss the order."

And they shook hands again. Bertram got a bit tangled up in Alexander's lace, which had hooked itself on to his watch, and there was brief confusion. (Vernon Brick watched all this from across the room, with the gloomy air of one who knew perfectly well that the lace was a hazard, and could have predicted this, if only anyone had been sensible enough to ask him.)

When he was untangled from Bertram's watch, Alexander took his leave, with a "Cheerio and *adieu*!" and an extravagant wave goodbye. He was a bit much, but Betsy liked him.

"Well," said Bertram. "Well, I never! Did you hear that, Grandad? Did you hear that, B?" He leaned against the table behind them, looking a bit dazed. "How do you think he knew about our party, eh?"

And it didn't feel like the sort of question that

anyone was meant to answer, so Betsy didn't. But Grandad looked at her with his eyebrows raised, because Grandad *always* knew.

When Bertram went off to tell Bella, Betsy did a little dance. "Can you believe it, Grandad? The Queen is going to eat our cakes!"

"Yes. In two days' time, apparently," said Grandad. "And I suspect, young lady, that the Royal Taster didn't find this party by accident. You and your Big Ideas!" And he wagged a finger at her, but his eyes were smiling. He picked up a fairy cake. "Eat up, B. We're going to need our strength for this one."

He was not wrong there.

CHAPTER FIVE

THE NIGHT OF MANY CAKES

The trouble with Big Ideas is that they tend to result in Big To-Do Lists, which in some serious cases can lead to Big Panic.

"I'm not panicking," Bertram told a worried Bella, when she tentatively suggested that maybe he *possibly* was, and asked if he was *certain* he wanted to do this. Betsy wasn't sure he was telling the truth, because as he said it, he was stirring with one hand and whisking with the other while

70

attempting to knead dough with his chin. But now was not the time to doubt him. Now was the time for the family to pull together, more than ever. She gave Bella a Look, and Bella nodded, and didn't ask again.

The not-a-panic had set in when Alexander Papparell had visited the morning after the party and dropped off the list of cakes he needed for the Gala, and it had seemed quite reasonable. Then he pointed out that the list was double-sided, and it seemed less reasonable. Then he had produced the lists of cakes for the Pre-Gala Reception, and the Post-Gala Ceremonial Tea, and the Post-Post-Gala Ceremonial Tea Reception. At which point Bertram had gone to have a little sit-down.

Then *another* man from the Palace had arrived to hand deliver their invitations to the Gala, in swirly gold writing. And when Bertram had seen these, he had pulled himself together and the action had begun.

Betsy was supposed to be piping, but so far she had mostly got the piping bag stuck to itself, and squirted icing and cream and custard all over her jumper and the lemon-yellow tablecloths. Because this time she didn't have the mice.

"Gaaaargh," said Betsy.

"Mind if I join you, B?" said Grandad. "I've done in the old elbows again – both at the same time, this time. Too much whisking." And he sat down at her table with a bag of frozen peas strapped to each arm, and took in the scene before him.

"Ah," he said. "No mice today."

"I thought I shouldn't. You know … with

Vernon…"

"Yes, of course," Grandad agreed. "I'm under

strict instructions to whisk these peas off if

he arrives. Can't have him deciding that the bakery is an elbow hazard."

Betsy put her head in her hands. This was a mistake, because now there was icing in her hair. "I can't do it," she mumbled into her palms. "Dad thinks I can do it. He doesn't know it was the mice. I have to go and tell him."

Grandad put an arm round her shoulder, which was nice, but also very chilly because of the frozen peas. "Yes, B," he said. "I think you do. But chin up. It's just piping bags."

So Betsy gathered her courage, and went into the kitchen. It was swelteringly hot in there, and every surface seemed to be sweating grease and the sticky remains of dough. Bertram was covered in flour from head-to-toe. Bella was shaping pastry as fast as she could manage, but her painfully stiff fingers had got worse, and she kept having to take breaks to flex and massage them before soldiering on. They all needed a day's rest to recover, but there was no time.

"Dad," said Betsy.

"Mm, yes, hmm? Quite," said Bertram.

"Dad." Betsy stood in front of him, to help him concentrate.

"Hello, B. Jolly good."

"I need to tell you something."

"Righto. I'm all ears. How's the piping going?" He smiled, but he was stirring with alarming vigour.

"Well, that's kind of what I wanted to talk about." Betsy took a deep, cakey breath. "Not very well. Dad, it was the mice doing it before. Not me. They were very clean about it, I promise. But still, I thought they might get you into trouble with Vernon, so I left them at home today. And I've been trying to do it myself, I promise I've really tried, but I can't do it."

Bertram just kept stirring and nodding and blinking, like a wind-up toy.

"Sorry, Dad," said Betsy. And she sounded so miserable that it finally snapped Bertram out of his trance. He actually stopped working for a moment, and gave her a floury hug.

"Don't worry about it, B," he said. "We'll

find a way to get it all done in time. Thank you for telling me." Then he looked as close to stern as he knew how, and added, "But no more secret mice in my bakery. Promise?"

Betsy promised, and after that, it really did seem to be all right. Well, mostly. True, Bella's worried frown got more worried than ever, and she had to take herself home for a quick cup of tea and a finger-bath and a deep breath before she could carry on. And then when she got back, she and Grandad did some worried whispering for *ages* in the front of the shop. And *then* Grandad somehow managed to whack his knee on the wall as well as his elbows, and had to go home for some more frozen peas. So they were obviously all a bit frazzled. But gradually they settled into a rhythm, and the pile of cakes grew and grew.

Betsy was now assigned to cracking eggs and stirring things, which was much better than icing. She got especially good at the eggs – the crack-*splosh* was very satisfying – and it was soothing to feel the dough thickening as she stirred. It felt like a magic spell going right.

While they worked, the sky outside darkened. It darkened some more. It finished darkening, and then just stayed dark. It was gone midnight by the time the last batch of cakes was rising in the oven.

There was no time for triumph. A mountain of cakes were waiting to be iced; a mountain of pastry cases were waiting to be filled with cream or custard or gooey chocolate. The family had a hasty late dinner of warm *pain au chocolat*, massaged their elbows and fingers, then turned in a daze to the piping bags.

Bertram was excellent at piping, of course.
Bella was good too, when her aching fingers
allowed. Grandad was even worse than Betsy,
and somehow managed to pipe a blob of
cream into his own eye.

They worked as fast as they could, but it wasn't fast enough – not even close. An hour in, Betsy looked at the pile of finished cakes, and the pile of waiting cakes, and put down her piping bag.

"We aren't going to be finished in time."

"Everything's fine, don't worry, yes, jolly good," said Bertram.

"No, it's not," said Betsy. "Look how many we've done so far."

They all looked.

"Look how many there are to do."

They all looked.

"We need to use the mice," said Betsy.

"No no, no need," said Bertram. "We just need to work faster. I can work faster. It's fine."

"Yes," said Bella, cradling her right hand in her left. "I could speed up. Probably. I can try."

"I can't," said Grandad. "I'm pretty sure I'm currently going in reverse. Surely humanity has come up with something better than piping bags? We've sent people to the moon, but we haven't come up with a way to pipe goop without getting our nostrils stuck together."

Since only Grandad had experienced this particular difficulty, they all just nodded.

Betsy tried again. "Dad, you'd need to work ten times as fast. At least."

"Maybe we could rewire the Mega-mix-o-matic to do it?" said Bertram, eyeing the machine uncertainly.

"Or we could just use the mice," said Betsy.

"Maybe we could ask some friends," said Bella. "Although it's very late…"

"Or," said Betsy, "we could just use the mice."

"Betsy's right," said Grandad.

"Or –" began Betsy automatically – then her brain caught up with what Grandad had said.

"I know you don't want to, Bertram," said Grandad. "But this will still be your achievement. The mice will just provide the icing on the cake, as it were. And Vernon isn't likely to inspect you at this time of night."

"He said any time of day *or night*," protested Bertram. "He was very keen to stress that."

"Well, I don't think he will, but if you like I'll keep watch at the window," said Grandad, "and tell you if he's coming. And if he does, Betsy can be out of the door with those mice lickety-split."

Betsy nodded, trying to look as lickety-splittish as she could.

"It's either that, or we don't finish the order," said Grandad. "If you want to choose not to finish, I'd understand. It's *your* bakery, and we don't have to do this Gala. But Betsy's right – we won't finish without the mice. We have to choose."

Bertram looked from Grandad to Betsy to Bella, to the pile of cakes, to the square of night sky in the window, and finally down at his feet.

"All right," he sighed. "Let's get the mice."

Betsy didn't need telling twice. She zoomed home with Bertram, who waited outside – "I need some air, B. Just a minute to breathe." So she zoomed by herself into the parlour, called the mice into their carry case, and zoomed back out into the hall.

That was when she noticed the answering machine, winking at her from the table. A message. She stopped in the dark hallway to play it back, just in case it was something important, like an update from the Palace.

It wasn't; it was just a friend calling for Bella. But then the machine blooped and went on to play its older messages, and this time, there *was* something from the Palace:

"Hello, this is Sarah from Buckingham Palace, returning Bella Bow-Linnet's call regarding the Gala," said a very polished voice. "Bella, I sympathize with your difficulties, but it would be *very* inconvenient for you to cancel at such short notice. We expect you to meet your commitments. Please call us back to discuss, on 0202 176982. Thank you, bye." Then there was a smart click, and nothing more.

Betsy stood frozen. Her mother had tried to *cancel* their delivery?

"Message finished. Second message," said the machine's recorded voice – and then Sarah was back again.

"Mr Bow. This is very disappointing news. I don't think you realize what difficulties your family are causing. Please call me back to discuss. Thanks."

Mr Bow? *Grandad* had called as well? Did neither of them believe that Bertram could do this?

She remembered Bella coming home to rest her fingers, and Grandad coming home for peas. And all their secretive whispering! The memory of their frowning and muttering filled her with a hot fury now. How *could* they have had so little faith? The family was supposed to stick together – and this was her dad's big chance. They were supposed to believe in him.

He mustn't know about this. Betsy put the mice down and replayed the messages, scribbling down the phone number, then jabbed the delete button three times, then a fourth for good measure. She picked up the phone and dialled the number, praying that she would only get an answering machine at this time of night. The dialling tone buzzed. Her heart skittered.

It *was* an answering machine. After the beep, she did her best impression of her mother:

"Hello, this is Bella Bow-Linnet," she lied. "I'm sorry about saying we would cancel. We definitely one hundred per cent won't. You can ignore my granda— I mean, my father, too. Goodbye. Um. Thanks."

That done, Betsy still wanted to do more, like start an argument, or kick something, or possibly cry. But none of this was useful, and she didn't want her dad to know that anything was wrong. So she just breathed deeply instead, and tried not to think about it.

When she stepped outside, Bertram was looking up at the moon. It seemed to have made him a little calmer, and when he turned to her, he looked more like himself. "Well done, B," he said. "What took you so long?"

Betsy swallowed. She didn't want to keep secrets – but it was Bella and Grandad who had started it, and there was nothing she could do about it now. "One of the mice had escaped," she lied. "Got them all now."

"Splendid," said Bertram, as firmly as he could. "Let's go then."

So they went, Betsy trying very hard to pretend she was still cheerful, as they walked back to their bakery under the watchful moon. It had begun to wane, and it wasn't a lucky half-moon any more. But the mice squeaked encouragingly from their carry case, and they were all the luck Betsy needed.

Probably.

CHAPTER SIX

INSPECTION

Bella and Grandad were waiting for them
eagerly, looking so earnest and encouraging
that Betsy felt hot tears starting. She couldn't
look at them. So she concentrated instead
on the mice, who were squeaking in ecstasy
at the good smells from the kitchen. While
Grandad went to keep watch at the window,
Betsy set the mice to work.

"Remember what we practised," she said,
putting her face level with the case. "Wash

your paws first."

Bertram watched them unhappily as they scurried around the piping bags. But soon they were finishing cakes at lightning speed, and he began to cheer up. It was hard *not* to be cheered up by the mice, when they squeaked so merrily, and blinked so brightly, and wiggled their whiskers at you.

"Aren't they *clever*," said Bella.

Betsy ignored her.

They were mostly very well behaved. Only D-flat-to-D second octave really didn't get the hang of it; he had an unfortunate sweet tooth,

 and kept trying to nibble the pastries. She banned him from the piping bags, but when she found him curled up

inside a strawberry bite, she had to put him back in the carry case by himself.

"You'll make yourself ill," she said sternly.

D-flat-to-D looked up at Betsy and twitched his shoulders, in what *might* have been a sulk.

"I'm sorry," she said. "But this is important."

By the time they were on the last batch of cakes, it was dawn. Even the mice were looking a bit droopy. They piped wearily, while Bertram and Bella dunked the last pastries into chocolate goop to give them a chocolate shell; Bertram was so tired that he was doing it with his eyes shut, which was quite impressive. But at last, the final pastry was gooped, and they were finished.

For a moment, the three of them just stared at the cakes in disbelief. The mice yawned happily, and cleaned their tails.

"We did it," said Bertram. He hugged Bella and Betsy. "*We did it.*"

That *we* stung Betsy, and made it hard to join in the celebration. The hot tears were beginning again. She blinked them away furiously, and ducked her mother's attempt at a hug. But before Bertram could notice that anything was wrong, Grandad called out from the window: "The van's here to collect the cakes! Ready in there? Time to load up!"

"*Perfect* timing," said Bella, giving Bertram a kiss.

"Thank goodness," said Bertram. "I thought he was going to say—"

"VERNON!" yelled Grandad. "Vernon Brick! He just drove up behind the van!"

So while Bertram and Bella hurried out to meet everyone, Betsy jumped into action, calling, "Home!" as she held the case out for her forty-four tiny chefs. Streaks of red flooded to the box and settled in happily.

"Well done," whispered Betsy. "And thank you." Forty-three noses twitched at her proudly. At least *they* were always on her team, whatever happened.

She had started to close the door before it hit her. She looked again. Forty-*three* noses.

The more she looked, the more there wasn't a forty-fourth. Where was D-flat-to-D?

At the front door, she could hear Vernon's voice already.

"Home. Home," she hissed – but D-flat-to-D did not appear. None of the mice had *ever* ignored home. Something was very wrong.

Footsteps were coming closer. Betsy realized, too late, that she had approximately three seconds until Vernon appeared, and that she wouldn't get to the back door in time. So she opened the bin, shoved the mice inside, and threw a tea towel on top.

Sqik, said the mice, which was fair enough.

"Shh," pleaded Betsy. Then Vernon opened the door to find Betsy *shh*ing a bin, so she thought quickly and turned it into, "*Shh*out for joy! Vernon's here!"

Vernon just straightened his tie and looked solemn, and a bit confused. This wasn't how inspections normally began. But it wasn't a hazard, exactly, so his gaze left Betsy and went wandering off around the kitchen.

While he gazed, the two van drivers came in behind him to collect the cakes, and began arming themselves with piles of trays. The Bow-Linnets hurried to help, all except Betsy, who was straining her ears for any squeak or scurry that might tell her where D-flat-to-D was.

"I shall begin," announced Vernon, to no one in particular, "with the refrigerator." And he went plodding off to the fridge like a menacing frog. He had a large grey bag full of mysterious equipment for testing things, and around his neck hung a Polaroid camera, the kind that prints out little square photos on the spot with a click-*whirrr*.

While he took a photograph of the fridge, Betsy listened. She edged nearer to the flour bags, and listened. She edged to the jars of chocolate and sprinkles and currants, and listened.

Nothing.

While she was listening to a sack of sugar, Grandad came in for more cakes, and paused.

"Everything all right, B?"

"Oh, yee-es," said Betsy, glancing over at
Vernon. His head was in a cupboard. Hastily,
she put a finger to the still-floury worktop,
wrote LOST MOUSE in the flour, then swept it
away again.

"Good, good, right," said Grandad. And
instead of picking up another tray, he
wandered casually over to the ovens, and

listened. Betsy listened to a microwave. Vernon peered into some copper-bottomed pans.

"Everything all right in here?" said Bella, coming in for more trays.

"Oh, yes, yes," said Grandad, dipping his finger in some leftover chocolate goop and writing LOST MOUSE on his forearm, then scrubbing it out into a gooey mess.

"Lovely," said Bella, nodding very slightly. And she wandered over to a tray of apple turnovers, and listened. Grandad listened to the dishwasher. Betsy listened to the spoon drawer. Vernon produced a magnifying glass and peered suspiciously at the sink.

"Erm," said one of the van drivers, coming in for more trays and looking round at the scene, "all OK in here?"

"FINE!" chorused three Bow-Linnets, while

Vernon responded that the sink was, overall, satisfactory. He proceeded to detail the finer points of plughole safety best practice. The driver looked like she regretted asking.

As though they were trapped in a dream, the four of them kept wandering about the kitchen, while around them Bertram and the van drivers bustled back and forth. The dream was interrupted by Bertram, as he picked up the almost-last trays.

"B," he said, gesturing to the last two trays. "Could you grab those? The drivers are in a bit of a hurry."

"Mm? Ah. Yes," said Betsy. She took the trays – it was the chocolate balls, the final tray which so recently had made them all hug each other for joy. Following Bertram outside, she was confused to find that the dawn had grown into a glorious spring morning. Then Vernon came plodding out behind them, so she hurried away from him and over to the van.

She didn't hear the squeak until she had handed the tray over to one of the drivers. It was very faint: no one else noticed. At first, Betsy couldn't place it.

Then it came again – and this time, with a sinking heart, she knew. It was coming from *inside* one of the pastries – the pastries that the driver was just putting in the van. D-flat-to-D must have curled up inside one before they were sealed up with chocolate.

"Oh, um, wait," she said. "I don't think that tray was meant to go."

"Yes, it was, B," said Bertram. He smiled cheerfully. "That's everything, I think?"

The driver checked his list. "Yup. We'll be on our way then."

"Really," said Betsy, her own voice squeaky now, "I think that tray was for us."

"Hungry, B?" said Bertram. "Come on. I'll make you fresh cookies for breakfast." As he spoke, the drivers were shutting the van doors.

Betsy got ready to throw a tantrum, which was not something she had much experience in. But just then, the bakery's telephone rang, and Bertram went hurrying off inside.

"That'll be the boss," said the driver, "checking everything's gone smoothly."

The second driver checked her watch. "He'll

be wondering where we are. Come on, let's get going."

"Please," said Betsy. "Wait. There's been a mistake…"

"No mistake," she said kindly, as she trotted round the side of the van and got into the cab. "Those are the Queen's cakes. I'd take your dad up on the cookies, if I were you."

And nothing Betsy could say would make them stop. She started yelling as the engine revved into life, but yelling couldn't halt the van as it drove away, filled to the brim with hundreds of cakes and pastries and biscuits and an accidental mouse.

Betsy watched them go, a hot wave of panic rising inside her. It had happened so *fast*. And all the while Vernon watched her, like a toad who has spotted a rebellious fly.

He came
plodding up
behind her, and
followed her gaze.
"What's the matter,
hmm?" he said. "Something wrong with those
cakes? Eh?"

"There's nothing wrong with any of it," said
Betsy hotly. "Please just *go away*."

Betsy had a feeling he was not going to forget
that, or forgive it. But it was too late to take it back.

"I will be the judge of that, young lady," he said. "For your information, I have already found an irregularity with the dishwasher prongs." He showed her his photograph of said prongs, and then of a wall, saying, "And this wall is an elbow hazard. You've passed, but there's plenty of room for improvement."

Betsy swallowed everything she wanted to say to this. What did Vernon Brick matter anyway, when D-flat-to-D was in a van, off to meet the Queen? She turned her gaze hopelessly to the empty road where the van had been, and now very much wasn't.

"And what's more," said Vernon, following her gaze, "I think this inspection is not over, is it? Hmm? What's worrying you? *What's wrong with those cakes?*"

Happily, they were interrupted by Bertram

coming back outside. "That was Mr Papparell, checking on the order." He rubbed his hands together happily. "What a success, eh, B? A real team, this family!"

Betsy looked at her floury father, and it took all her strength not to cry. He was wrong about them being a team, and that left nothing right at all. But she just nodded.

"Time," said Bertram, "for a celebratory breakfast!"

So they said goodbye to Vernon, who was too busy grumbling about suspicious cakes to say goodbye back, and they headed inside the bakery. Birds sang. Bertram whistled.

And Vernon Brick stood still and watched them go, eyes agoggle. Like a toad who is still hungry.

CHAPTER SEVEN

Buckingham Palace

When they were all back inside, Betsy told them what had happened in one frantic rush. Her anger had turned into a burning shame. This was all her fault, for insisting that they used the mice. They should have just admitted that they couldn't get it done in time, and not taken any stupid risks. Grandad and Bella had been right, after all.

It took everyone a moment to take in what she was saying. There was a lot of nodding, and a few thoughtful "*Hmms*".

"So just to be clear," said Bertram. "We have sent a mouse in the van. To Buckingham Palace."

Betsy nodded.

Bertram considered this, and said, "Ohhh. Ohhhnooooo."

Bella dithered, unsure who needed a hug most, and said, "Let's not panic. He'll probably just curl up asleep in a corner somewhere and no one will know. They are *very* tiny."

"You don't understand," said Betsy. "He's crawled *inside* the pastry case, and now he's stuck. They were covered in chocolate. The mice can't eat chocolate – it's poisonous – they're too smart to even try." It occurred to her for the first time to hope that this would still be true, and that D-flat-to-D wouldn't try in a panic – she didn't want to even think about that.

Bertram, who had been dipping those pastries with his eyes closed, realized what he had done, and updated his earlier remark to "Ohhh. Ohhhnononooooo*no*."

No one said anything to this. There wasn't much to say. And everyone needed a moment to themselves after the horrible thought of someone trying to eat their pastry, and discovering D-flat-to-D.

"Imagine," whispered Bella, "if the *Queen* tries to eat it."

This was one imagining too far for Bertram. He put his face in his hands. "We'll have to call and warn them."

"Dad!" cried Betsy. "You'd be shut down!"

"Still..."

"No way, nope, no, nope," said Betsy. She was saying it to convince herself as much as anybody: she was frantic with worry for the mouse, but she had to believe there was still a way to save the situation. If the bakery was closed down because of her Big Idea, she would never forgive herself. "I'll find a way to get D-flat-to-D back."

"That's the spirit," said Grandad. "No use standing around here like gormless lemons. We're the chefs – we must be able to find an excuse to get inside the palace kitchens."

Bertram took his face out of his hands again, and nodded slowly. "How about," he said, "I take the ... the silver balls, or something – and I say I forgot some of the decoration. And I can ask to be allowed in to fix the mistake."

"Brilliant!" said Grandad. "Genius! Foolproof! Let's get to it then. No time to lose."

So that is how it happened that the Bow-Linnets, who were so tired they kept walking into large pieces of furniture and forgetting the words for things, washed their faces and combed their hair and called a taxi instead of going to bed. They all put on their smartest clothes, because they were meant to be attending the Gala later, and wouldn't get a chance to change.

Betsy wanted to take the mice's carry case with her, for the rescued mouse, but the other mice refused to leave it. They knew that D-flat-to-D was missing, and they sat stubbornly with their claws digging in, determined to join the rescue party. In the end Betsy gave in and brought them along, the case safely hidden inside a big black bag. She felt better with them beside her, anyway.

Normally a taxi was a treat. Today, Betsy hardly noticed London slip past, or the fun foldy-down seats. She was too busy worrying about D-flat-to-D, alone in his pastry cage.

As they neared the Palace, the traffic thickened like dough, until they were moving unbearably slowly. With a couple of streets to go they stopped the taxi and ran the rest of the way. At last, panting enormously, they were standing in front of Buckingham Palace, Bertram clutching the jar of silver balls.

They looked at each other. They looked at the Palace.

"Right," said Bella. "How do we... I mean ... is there a bell we should ring?"

Betsy looked at the gates. They had black rails with gold tips and shields with lions and unicorns and also some cherubs and some more lions with crowns on. But they didn't seem to have a bell.

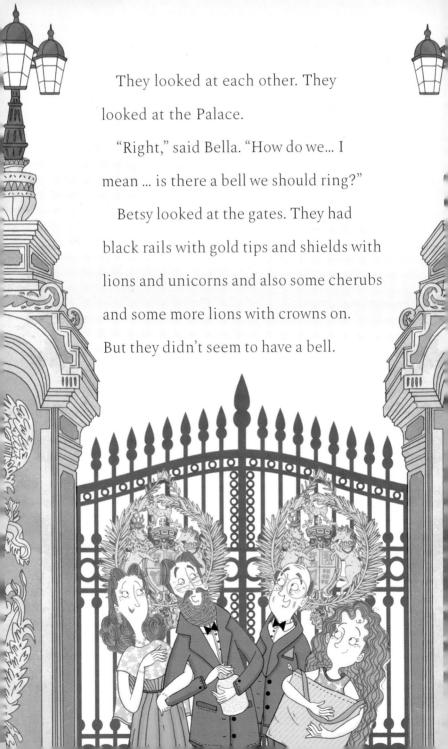

At the back of the forecourt, there were two guards in red. One stood still; the other was marching from left to right and then, with great aplomb, from right to left. Neither of them looked too busy.

"Excuse me!" called Bertram, face to the railings. "Sorry to bother you! Hello?" And then they all tried yelling "EXCUSE ME!" at once, in case the guards hadn't heard. But nobody excused them.

"There must be another way in," said Betsy, fizzing with impatience. "I'll go and look, I'll be right back." She set the mice down at her family's feet, and was trotting off before Grandad had finished saying "Good idea, B, I'll come with you", so he had to pump his elbows hard to catch her up.

They jogged all round the enormous palace, and at every door they knocked and knocked and knocked. It didn't make them any less shut. When they had gone almost all the way round they passed a twiddly gate leading to a small car park, and Betsy almost trotted right past it, before doing a double-take.

"*Grandad*," she said.

There, in the car park, was the van. The doors stood open.

They stopped and stared. They were so close. But they were also very much on the wrong side of the gate.

"Well," said Grandad, "we're hot on the trail then, B! Let me try this next door." And he ambled off to the left to try yet more knocking on the nearest door, while Betsy stood, transfixed. The van was *right there*. Was there no way to wriggle inside? She pushed her face to the railings, as though she could push herself through.

It all happened very fast after that.

First, a guard in a far archway spotted her, causing her to withdraw her face hastily.

Second, the guard called out, "Sarah!" and jerked his head at the gate. "I think Alice is here!"

And third, a woman came hurrying across the driveway looking stressed. "Alice O'Golly?" she said – and thankfully not waiting for a reply, she opened the gate, barking, "You're late! Come along!"

Sarah's voice would have been unmistakable, even if the guard hadn't said her name. It was the polished woman from the answering machine, and she looked as polished as she had sounded.

There was only a moment to decide what to do. Sarah was flapping impatiently, and if Betsy hesitated, she might want to double-check about the Alice thing. Betsy could feel her heart pounding, in her chest and her neck and her ears, and she stepped through the gates like someone in a dream.

But from inside the gates, she could see that the open van was empty. The cakes must already be inside the Palace. Which meant Betsy needed to be inside, too.

Sarah marched ahead, obviously much too busy and impatient to make any small talk with the girl she thought was Alice. Betsy had to hurry behind her at a quick trot to keep up. Before she stepped through the door into the Palace, she looked over her shoulder and saw that Grandad had just got back. He was staring at her, face pale, mouth and elbows flapping in alarm.

"B?" he called.

Betsy had to ignore this: the guard was still there and she could hardly respond to 'B' if she was meant to be Alice. So she turned away as though she didn't know him. It felt terrible, but he would understand later that she had made the right decision. Which she had. Probably. What was the punishment for going into Buckingham Palace under a false name? Betsy had no idea.

Then the door slammed shut behind her, and it was too late for doubts.

She had expected lots of gold and grandeur, but they were in the staff's corner of the palace. It was very plain, and full of people rushing about with trolleys in the corridors, and shouting into phones in the offices she passed. When one of the rushing-trolley people appeared through a door on their left, a rich smell suddenly burst into the corridor with them. Betsy craned her neck to see. The kitchen!

But she couldn't stop now. She took care to remember every twist and turn of the corridor after that, so that she could sneak back later. She didn't have much to remember: Sarah soon came to a halt, opened a door, and commanded, "In here. Stay until you're called for. There are sandwiches."

"Thank you," said Betsy.

But Sarah was already hurrying away, so Betsy slipped inside. She counted to ten to give Sarah time to get back to her office.

Meanwhile, she stared at the room, trying to work out who Alice was.

The room stared back. A string quartet were tuning their instruments, a singer was warbling up and down some scales, and a group of children were sitting in fairy ballet outfits. They must all be performing at the Gala, she decided. So Alice was some kind of performer then.

"Hello, dear," said the cellist from the quartet. "Are you another fairy?"

"She's not with *us*," said the nearest fairy, wrinkling his nose.

Betsy counted eight-nine-ten at double speed, and saying, "Oh, I'm here for something else – 'scuse me, got to find the toilets," she hurried from the room. She looked left. She looked right. Sarah was gone.

She hurried back along the corridor to the rich smell, and when she had found the right door, she peeped through its round window at the kitchen beyond. It was enormous, and a blur of activity.

It was going to be impossible to sneak in unnoticed. For a minute she just stood, watching chefs through the window as they flitted past.

Then, like a goldfish bowl that suddenly contains a piranha, the window was full of Alexander Papparell. He hadn't seen her yet, but he was walking right towards her – and then he was reaching out one lace-cuffed arm, and opening the door.

CHAPTER EIGHT

THE ROYAL KITCHENS

Betsy lurched away in a panic. She pulled
open the nearest door, which proved to be a
pantry full of tins, and flung herself into it.
It was mostly taken up with shelves, and she
couldn't get the door to close entirely with her
inside. But she would just have to keep it pulled
almost-shut and hope for the best, because
she could hear the kitchen door opening and
Alexander Papparell stepping out.

He was with another man, who unfortunately

seemed to be in no hurry, and parked himself outside Betsy's cupboard for a chat. She breathed very, very quietly.

"Well, well, *well*," said the other man. "I'm impressed, Alexander. Those cakes of yours really are delicious. What *is* the secret?"

Betsy was still concentrating on breathing quietly, but a corner of her brain thought: cakes of *yours*?

"Oh, no secret, no secret," said Alexander. Although she couldn't see him, she could hear the wafting of the lacy cuffs. "Just some hard work. But I am delighted you approve, Pedro."

"I *don't* approve," said Pedro, chuckling. "You're an excellent secretary, and I don't want to lose you! But my conscience says I *must* put you forward for Royal Baker now, on my honour as Royal Taster. And once the Queen tastes your fabulous cakes, I fear she will agree."

Alexander Papparell murmured modestly, and swished his lace. Betsy stayed silent, but inside she was furious. He was taking the credit for *their* cakes! After all their hard work! And on top of that, he wasn't even really the Royal Taster. They had been tricked.

"But come on, really, Alexander," said Pedro. "What's the secret? You've always been good, but these are exceptional!"

The lace-swishing got more agitated, as Alexander protested a little too loudly that it was just hard work and practice and of course Pedro's wise feedback and oh *goodness*, is that the time already? And it *was* the time already, and Pedro went hurrying off down the corridor. When he had gone, Alexander let out an enormous sigh of relief and leaned back against

Betsy's cupboard.

"Ooof," said the cupboard – or so it must have seemed to Alexander, who jumped back in alarm. Of course, what really said *ooof* was a girl who didn't really fit in a small pantry, and now had a squashed foot and a bashed knee and a knocked funny bone.

Betsy bit her lip, but it was too late to keep that *ooof* inside. She waited, breath held.

There was a pause. Then, cautiously, the pantry door opened, and Alexander Papparell's face fell in horrified astonishment.

"What," he hissed, "are *you* doing here?"

"Overhearing *you*," said Betsy, "you liar."

She gave her funny bone a vigorous rub and stepped out of the pantry. They glared at each other.

"You don't have permission to be here," said Alexander, at the same moment as Betsy said, "You're lying about Dad's cakes." More glaring.

"I'm going to tell someone," said Betsy, as Alexander said, "I'm going to call the guard."

Alexander's lace trembled and he dropped the glare. "Look," he said, "I'll do you a deal. I'll get you out of here quietly, if you promise not to tell anyone." And since Betsy was still glaring, he added, "I *am* going to pay your father. And I'll never do anything like this again. The Royal Baker is retiring, you see, so this is my big audition."

"That doesn't make it all right."

Alexander thought about this. "Doesn't it?" he said – then, hopefully, "Not even a little bit?"

Betsy collected her thoughts. There wasn't time for this. D-flat-to-D was still trapped, and she needed to rescue him. Alexander could help her there – and, she realized, he would *have* to help her.

"Look," she said, "forget that a minute. I'm here because there's a mouse in one of those cakes— "

There was a *lot* of lace-swishing and spluttering from Alexander at that.

"Oh, calm down," said Betsy, "it's only a small one. And you're going to help me get him out of there, because everyone thinks they're *your* cakes."

Alexander's face went through astonishment and disgust and horror at lightning speed, as he took all this in. He checked his watch. "Oh lord – the first lot will be going up for the Pre-Gala Reception any minute. Fine, fine. I'll say you're with me. Look casual."

They hurried into the
kitchen, Betsy looking casual,
and Alexander looking like a
puppet that hasn't been very
well designed for walking. He
lurched through the kitchen with
a fixed grin on his face, beaming
and nodding at everyone they
passed. Betsy began to wonder
if she would have been better
off without him. But it worked.
With his hand on her shoulder, no
one questioned whether she was
allowed to be there.

He led Betsy through the hustle
and bustle to an enormous walk-in
pantry, then shut the door.

"Well," he said. "Go on."

It took Betsy a minute to find the little chocolate balls, but once she had, it only took a moment to find D-flat-to-D. He was muffled by the pastry, but with her ear close, Betsy could make out that he was squealing frantically. She picked up the pastry and it trembled on her palm.

"Shh," she whispered. "It's me. You're safe. Shhhhh."

The pastry grew still. *Sqik?* it said.

"That's right," Betsy whispered. Then, more loudly, she said, "Wow, thanks for my treat, Mr Papparell."

Alexander, who had been watching the shuddering pastry with alarm, nodded slowly. He opened the door, eyes still fixed on the pastry, and said loudly,

"You're very welcome. You enjoy that cake now. I'll show you out."

But no one was listening to their pantomime, because they were all very busy with a kerfuffle happening in the kitchen. At the centre of the kerfuffle stood a man with a large grey bag in one hand and a Polaroid camera around his neck. He was straightening his tie, and swivelling his great eyes around the kitchen.

Betsy's fingers closed protectively around the pastry. What was Vernon Brick doing here?

CHAPTER NINE
THE GREAT MOUSE CHASE

"Those cakes are suspicious items," he was saying, "and I have every right to inspect them. I am the *Chief* Health and Safety Inspector for—"

"I don't care if you're Her Majesty the Queen," fumed a man with an extra-large chef's hat. "This is *my* kitchen, and I'm in charge in here. I won't have interruptions."

Vernon ignored him, because he had seen Betsy. "A*ha*! *You!* What's wrong with those cakes, then?" He pointed a finger accusingly. "She's from the family that made those cakes! I *must* insist—"

"Well, *I* must make a white sauce, and you're wasting my time," said the head chef. "Alexander made those cakes. You've made some mistake. If you don't get out of my kitchen this minute..."

"You?" said Vernon to Alexander, blinking stupidly. "But aren't you the Royal Ta—?"

"A misunderstanding!" cried Alexander loudly. "Let me take you to my office and explain." And he flung out an inviting arm towards the kitchen door.

This was an error.

A nervous young chef carrying a pot full of soup got a face full of Alexander's arm, including a lot of lace up his nose. "Nnf" he objected, as soup spilled everywhere.

Alexander withdrew his arm in horror, and the unfortunate chef stepped forward, only to slip on his own soup and stagger into Betsy, who stumbled – and dropped the pastry, which splattered open on the floor.

In the general pandemonium, the chefs weren't paying any attention to the little pastry. But Vernon was.

"MOUSE!" he roared. "MOUSE IN A CAKE! It's a hazard! It's a rodent! It's an abomination!"

D-flat-to-D, covered in chocolate goop and crumbs from the exploded pastry, shot through the kitchen and out of the door. Betsy reached out a desperate hand, but she was much too slow.

The head chef was towering over Vernon now. "Sir. There is not, and never has been, and never will be, a mouse in the Royal Kitchens. However, there is a lot of soup and upset, and this is *precisely* why we cannot have any interruptions…"

Betsy didn't wait to hear more. By unspoken agreement, she and Alexander made for the door.

Ahead, there was a confused *Sqik*? – and there was D-flat-to-D, looking right at them. Behind him, a trolley was being wheeled into an open lift. The man with the trolley, thankfully, had his back to them. Betsy knelt down, and held out a pleading hand.

But before the mouse could come, Vernon burst out from the kitchen. "THERE!" he roared. "Mouse! And it's still covered in crumbs! PROOF!"

And with one last terrified squeak, D-flat-to-D whisked away into the lift – the doors shut – and the lift moved off, upwards into the Palace, man and trolley and mouse on board.

For a moment, Betsy, Alexander and Vernon were all frozen, staring at the place where the mouse had been. Then, as though someone had fired a starting gun, all three of them were off, in the strangest race Betsy had ever known.

She and Alexander had a head start, because some of the less-flustered chefs realized they probably shouldn't let Vernon wander off into the Palace, and tried to hold him back. He had to waste time showing them his License to Inspect and persuading them to let him go. This gave the others an advantage, but Betsy knew Vernon would get his way in the end. So when Alexander hissed, "The stairs," she followed him double-quick.

They had to slow to a more sedate walk in a hallway full of open office doors, trying to look casual. As they walked, from one office she heard: "Sarah, that was Alice's mother on the phone. You know, the little girl who was meant to sing at the Gala? She's sick."

"But she's already here," said Sarah's voice. As soon as they were out of that hallway, Betsy raced up the stairs two at a time.

On the next floor, the lift stood open and empty. For a moment she and Alexander both stared at it. Then Vernon came panting up behind.

"Gone, eh?" he said. "Unimportant. I'll find it." And from his grey bag he produced a little black stick, which looked like a remote control, but with fewer buttons. He turned it on and a red light blinked solemnly. "Rodent detector," he explained. "This won't take long." And giving them both a ghastly, triumphant smile, he made his way down the corridor, waving the detector from left to right.

"He," whispered Alexander, "is a very unpleasant man."

Betsy nodded. "Alexander, we *have* to find my mouse before he does. You know the Palace. Which way?"

"Right, right," said Alexander. "Yes. Of course. In here." And he opened a door to their left.

"But he can't have gone through a closed—" began Betsy – and then she stopped, because she was interrupted by an excited chorus of Somethings.

Yip yip yip yip, they said.

Alexander plunged into the room. "Oof – come here – *bad* – ow – gotcha!" he said, and emerged with a little brown dog yipping in his arms. Betsy stared. The Queen's corgi dogs were famous, but she had always imagined they would be more – well – royal.

Yip, announced the corgi, flapping its tail.

"Excellent mousers," explained Alexander.

"Absolutely not, no way, nope," said Betsy. "We need to find my mouse *alive*."

Alexander considered this. "We'll put him on a lead," he bargained, "so he can't get the mouse. But he'll know if he's nearby, and get excited."

Betsy wasn't sure. It still seemed risky. And the corgi was currently chewing like crazy on Alexander's lace, which wasn't encouraging.

"Betsy," pleaded Alexander, "it's the fastest way by far. Vernon's got his detector thingummybob. We can't search the whole Palace for a mouse just by looking."

"OK," said Betsy, "but use a *really* short lead."

So with the corgi on a red-and-gold lead, yipping furiously, the race began in earnest.

Up here, the Palace was much more as Betsy had imagined. Enormous rooms in red and gold and duck-egg-blue led to yet more enormous rooms, and all of them had chandeliers and paintings and vases and statues and unfriendly curly chairs.

The corgi was very excited by this unexpected outing. In a huge red room, he excitedly chased his own tail. In a huge gold room, he excitedly chased a bit of dust. In a huge duck-egg-blue room, he excitedly tried to knock over a table with a crystal globe on it, which provoked a lot of bad words and lace-swishing from Alexander. But none of his excitement led them to a mouse.

Betsy wished she had the case; then she could just call the mouse home. But she had left it with her parents. She thought of her family now, waiting worriedly outside with her mice, and hoped she wasn't making this whole mess worse.

The rooms were a maze, each one opening out on to at least two more. Sometimes they would hear Vernon's plodding footsteps in a nearby room, and Betsy's heart rate would double. She wished she could have the corgi's sharp ears. Every slight breath of air seemed to her like it could be a mouse.

The maze seemed endless, but at last they reached a dead end, a corner room that didn't lead anywhere else. It was a huge red room full of bronze busts, and it had been filled with cakes and champagne bottles and flowers. There were rows of seats facing a grand piano. It must, Betsy guessed, be the room for the Gala.

Then the corgi went berserk.

He was straining desperately for one of the bronze busts, which sat on a pillar near the door.

It was marked *Prince Alphonse the Nice*.
Betsy and Alexander looked at each other.

"Investigate," said Alexander, scooping
up the corgi. "I'll hold him back."

So, quietly, slowly, Betsy peered around
Alphonse the Nice. And there, at the base
of the pillar, sat a quivering speck of red-
and-brown fur, still covered in bits of
chocolate and pastry. Betsy had never seen
a mouse cry, but she thought she might
be looking at it now. D-flat-to-D
was scared out of his mind.

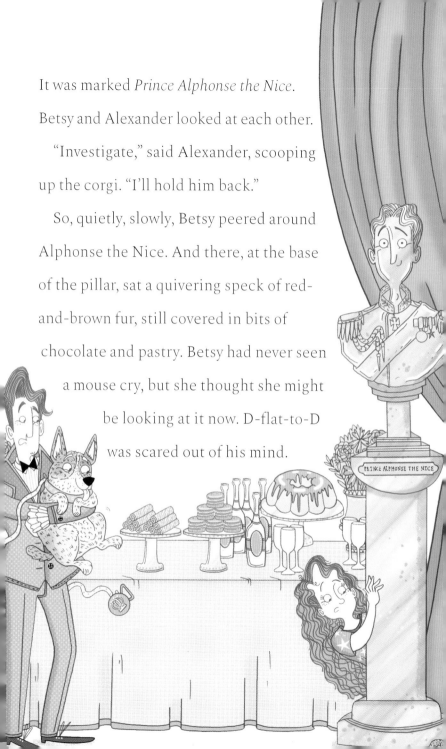

PRINCE ALPHONSE THE NICE

"Here," she said softly, holding out a hand.

D-flat-to-D trembled.

"Hey. It's me."

A nose poked cautiously out of the fur, and sniffed. Then, with a squeak of joy, the tiny mouse hurried on to Betsy's hand.

She stood up, holding her palm out carefully, for Alexander to see. "See," she said, "they're really *very* small. But people always make a fuss."

And as if to prove her right, at that moment, there was a smug click-*whirrr* from the doorway, and Vernon Brick's camera began to print his picture of Betsy and Alexander and D-flat-to-D. Before they could react, he leaned in for a close-up of the chocolatey mouse.

"The size of the rodent," he explained gravely, "is not important. If it was the size of a pin, I would still be shutting down your bakery."

While Betsy gaped at him in horror, he turned to Alexander. "As for you, I don't know why you are claiming responsibility for these cakes, or helping this girl, but I will get to the bottom of it. I am going to show these photos to the head chef – and if he won't listen, I'm taking it to Her Majesty. Those cakes must be thrown out."

"Please," said Betsy. "You can't—" But as she was speaking, Vernon left and shut the door – and there was another *click*, but a different kind this time. A lock turning.

Betsy tugged at the handle. It was no use.

"I *can*," came Vernon's voice, from the other side of the door. "You seem to forget, young lady, that I am the Chief Health and Safety Inspector for the Greater London Area."

And with that, Vernon Brick went plodding off in triumph. The race was over.

CHAPTER TEN

ONE LAST BIG IDEA

Betsy kicked the door.

"Betsy," began Alexander, "that door was a gift from the Princess of—"

She gave him a Look.

"Never mind," he said.

But Betsy stopped kicking the door anyway, because it was making the mouse on her shoulder wobble, and he was squeaking in alarm. She wanted to sob great heaving sobs, but she was worried the little mouse would fall right off. So she screwed up her fists and her face, and willed the sobbing swell inside her to go away.

Alexander looked a bit concerned.

"Um," he said, "are you all..." And then faltered, because she obviously wasn't all right. He tried again. "Betsy, I'll make sure I take the blame for this. We can think up some story." And he wafted his lace at her, with the half-hearted gesture of someone who knows about hugs in theory, but isn't really sure how to go about them. Still, he was trying.

"Thanks," said Betsy, pushing a very small voice out of her screwed-up face. "But there isn't anything you could say. The bakery is getting shut down." And then, even though Alexander was being nice, bitter words swelled out as though she had sprung a leak and couldn't stop. "We all worked so hard. I really thought the Royal Taster had read my letter. I was so *stupid*. And it was my idea, and using the mice was my idea, and my mum and my grandad tried to call it off because they could see how stupid it all was. And now I've ruined everything."

At this Alexander looked *very* concerned and wafty, but a bit lost for words. Betsy had said all of her words for now, so she just sank to the floor and wrapped her arms round her knees. He sat down beside her. Alphonse the Nice smiled nicely down at them, and the corgi settled next to Alexander for a nap after all the excitement.

"I truly am sorry," said Alexander. "I convinced myself it was all right – your father would be paid handsomely, and I would be Royal Baker at last, and nobody would get hurt. But I think I knew deep down that it wasn't all right, and … well, I'm sorry."

It didn't seem to matter very much either way now. So Betsy said, in her new small voice, "'Salright." And D-flat-to-D came scurrying to the edge of Betsy's shoulder to twitch his nose at Alexander in a friendly and encouraging way. Even though he was still drooping sadly all over, the tiny mouse made him smile.

"I'm glad we rescued him," he said. "He's lovely. How did he end up inside a cake?"

"It's a long story," sighed Betsy.

Alexander wafted at the locked door. "Well," he said, "we're not going anywhere."

This was true, so Betsy started talking, mostly to stop herself thinking. And once she had started, she just kept going. She told him about all the adventures of the mice, everything from the cake shop to the circus to the Royal Albert Hall to Mrs Fortesque's hoover. Normally she enjoyed telling these stories, but now for the first time it struck her that they were all just stories of how she and her mice caused a lot of trouble for everyone else. Her family always helped her get out of it, only for her to repay them with more trouble.

She thought of Grandad gaping at her, pale and horrified, as she had walked into the Palace with the cocky idea that she could fix everything. She felt so ashamed.

Alexander's mouth had fallen open in astonishment quite early in the story, and as Betsy kept saying more and more astonishing things, he just kept it open. When she had finished he shut it at last, and looked in wonder at the mouse on her shoulder.

"Remarkable," he said, lace aflutter. "What extraordinary creatures. And," he added, "you seem quite extraordinary yourself."

"I don't want to be," said Betsy. "I'm going to start being really, really, really ordinary, and stop causing trouble with my stupid Big Ideas."

"That seems like a shame," said Alexander, "because now would be an excellent time for you to have one. The Gala is happening here in fifteen minutes, and I don't have any ideas at all."

Betsy shut her eyes. "Oh, I don't want to think about it. My family are coming. Walking right into all this."

Alexander looked a bit startled at that. "Are they?"

"Of course," said Betsy. And then it suddenly struck her as odd, and she opened her eyes again. "Wait," she said. "Why did you invite us, if you were lying about who baked the cakes?"

"I most certainly *didn't* invite you," said Alexander. "For that very reason."

Betsy couldn't make *any* sense of this. She thought it over for a minute, but it didn't get her anywhere. And she was so tired of thinking: her head ached and her eyes were hot with exhaustion and worry. She wanted to shut out her thoughts, just for a minute.

She closed her eyes again. "Your turn to explain, Alexander. Why do you want to be Royal Baker so much? Let's have *your* story."

"Er," said Alexander, a bit taken aback, as though it had never occurred to him that he *had* a story. "Well, there's not much to tell."

Betsy waited.

"OK, um," said Alexander, stroking the corgi for encouragement. "Well, I suppose it started because I've always loved baking. My granny taught me, and she used to think I was smashing – she said I'd cook for the Queen one day. And, well, I wasn't much good at anything else. That was all a long time ago now. Since then, my brother has grown up to be a very important lawyer, and my sister has grown up to be a very important banker, and my other sister is a top scientist at the British Space Programme. And I was just a baker." Alexander paused. "Is this what you meant? It's rather boring."

"I'm listening."

"OK. Well. They all look down on me, and since my granny died – I suppose I've felt quite lonely. And I had this dream that if I could bake for the Queen I'd be doing her proud, and maybe then the others wouldn't be so snobby to me. I kept sending cakes to the Palace, but they said they couldn't accept them in case they were going to poison the Queen or something. So when I had the opportunity for a job with the Royal Taster, I quit my job at a bakery and took it – I thought it would give me a chance to finally show him what I could do." He sighed. "It didn't work, obviously. He tried my cakes, and he agreed that they were good, but he already had a Royal Baker – so that was that. It was a stupid plan."

"It wasn't a stupid plan!" said Betsy. "It sounds like a good plan. It just didn't work out, that's all."

Alexander smiled at her then, a proper smile. "Is that so? It's funny, I can think of somebody else who could use that advice."

And Betsy had to smile back at that. She found she wasn't really cross with Alexander, now he had apologized so sincerely. She even found she liked him better now that he wasn't pretending to be the Royal Taster. He waved his lace less wildly, and he wasn't always using three words where one would do.

"So," she prompted. "You were trying one more time?"

"Yes," said Alexander. "The Royal Baker's retiring, and I'm in the final three candidates to take over the job. This was my big audition.

I've been losing sleep over it for weeks. And then I came to your party – I always take up any invitations to try cakes, for research – my boss isn't interested. And your cakes were simply the best I have *ever* tasted. I knew if I served those, I was *guaranteed* to get the job."

There was a short silence, then he added, "I'm sorry. It was wrong. I was so obsessed with finally making my family proud, instead of just being any old baker."

"But you *liked* being a baker," said Betsy. "I think you should go back to doing that, if you liked it."

"Maybe." He sighed. Then he chuckled. "Do you know, my name isn't really Alexander Papparell. It's Alexander Pepper. I just panicked when I was introducing myself, and stuck the 'ell' bit on to sound fancy."

"That," said Betsy, "is mad."

"Look who's talking," said Alexander. "This is the girl who claims she has forty-four mice that can all play the piano."

"They *can*!" said Betsy. Alexander was smiling, so she knew he was only teasing her, but still she was indignant. "I'd show you," she said, "if I had the others. He can't really do it by himself."

Then she said, "Oh," because she had just had another Big Idea. But she wasn't supposed to be having any more.

This was what she had realized: one mouse alone was a hazard, with no good excuse for being inside Buckingham Palace. But *forty-four mice* were a piano-playing spectacular. Alice was sick. If Betsy could convince everyone that the mice were here to replace Alice, then she and D-flat-to-D would have a perfectly good reason to be in here. They could deny Vernon's whole story about mice-cakes and break-ins.

"Alexander," she said, "I think I might see a way out of this."

His face lit up. "Really?"

"Yes. But … maybe it's silly. It *feels* like a good idea. But they always do, in the beginning, and then they go wrong."

"Betsy," said Alexander, "the only way to never ever get anything wrong is to not do anything, ever. And if we don't do anything on this occasion, in about the next seven minutes," he added, "then the Gala guests will find us here, and we are all in very deep trouble."

Yip, said the corgi sleepily.

"All right," Alexander agreed, "you're probably not. But the rest of us are."

"OK," said Betsy, "I'll tell you the idea, and you can tell me if you think it's good. You need to be honest. I don't want to make things any worse."

"*Could* we make things worse?"

"I don't know." said Betsy. "Maybe. Right now there's only one mouse in here." And she smiled, because deep in her belly, it *did* feel like a good idea. "How do you feel about forty-three more?"

CHAPTER ELEVEN

THE ROYAL GALA

Betsy sat on the piano stool, trying to look like someone who is attending a Royal Gala on purpose. D-flat-to-D scurried into the piano. Alexander stood ready at the door. They waited in tense silence. If Vernon arrived with a witness before Betsy's family came in with the rest of the mice, the plan was over.

To their relief, before Vernon reappeared there was a crowded clatter of footsteps, and a swell of voices: the Gala guests were arriving.

There was a brief moment of confusion about the locked door, then a footman murmured – there was a *click* – and it opened.

Hats sailed into the room. In among the hats were three worried faces Betsy knew. She felt a pang of guilt, and sincerely hoped she wasn't about to make things worse again.

"Hello," said Alexander brightly, as Bertram walked past him with the large black bag. "I'll have this, please."

"Er," said Bertram. But Alexander had already taken the bag and was handing it to Betsy, who opened it on the belly of the piano.

"Play," she hissed, and the mice ran to their places – just in time. As they were whisking down to the piano strings, a footman by the door called "Ladies and gentlemen!", and all the ladies and gentlemen stopped talking at once.

YIP, yip yip! said the corgi, who was having a very exciting dream behind one of the statues.

The footman heroically ignored this. "Her Majesty," he announced, "Queen Elizabeth the Second!"

Then the Queen herself came into the room, and everybody bowed. Betsy hastily stood and bowed too. Her heart hammered. Suddenly this seemed like a very, very stupid plan.

They all waited for the Queen to take a seat before sitting themselves. Then the footman announced, "We will now enjoy some musical entertainment." It sounded like a command.

Everybody looked at Betsy, including the Queen. They all looked polite, but also like they would probably rather be looking at the delicious cakes waiting on the tables – *especially* the Queen. Betsy took a deep breath.

"Her!" came a voice from the back of the room. "That's the girl!"

The hats all swivelled in surprise to look at Vernon Brick, who was goggling from the doorway, with Sarah in tow.

"Hazard!" cried Vernon, addressing the crowd now and pointing at Betsy. "Danger! Aider and abettor of rodents!"

"I'm very, very, very sorry, Your Majesty," said Sarah, blushing deeply. "But that girl isn't supposed to be performing."

The hats swivelled back to Betsy.

Betsy felt much too hot, and her heart was now pulsing in her ears in a very distracting way. But if she wanted anyone to believe what was coming next, the most important thing was to look confident.

"But I thought you knew, Sarah?" she said.

She did her very best Innocent Face. "I'm the replacement."

"Replacement?" repeated Sarah.

"I'm afraid I took the phone call, Sarah, and forgot to tell you," said Alexander. "My mistake. This young lady has agreed to step in at short notice."

"Lies!" declared Vernon, waving his photos in the air. "I have evidence, here, of that girl sneaking about with a mouse!"

"There must be some misunderstanding," said Betsy, blinking at him. "I don't have one mouse."

"Yes, you d—"

"I have forty-four."

Vernon stopped at this, the 'oo' still on his lips, and his eyes bulged wildly. Sarah looked helplessly at the footman, who shrugged.

"They are here," said Betsy, "to play the piano for you all. Mice! Bow!" And on the command, forty-four mice came out on to the piano lid, and bowed hello to the crowd. A bit of chocolate quivered off D-flat-to-D. "I am afraid one of them is a little messy," said Betsy. "Mr Pepper kindly gave him a cake for a treat."

She held her breath, and watched the Queen. If people started screaming and standing on chairs and being silly about it, she was in just as much trouble as ever. But no one wanted to scream or stand on chairs or any of that until they knew what the Queen thought about it all. All hats were swivelled to Her Majesty.

The Queen was leaning forwards, looking at the mice. She mostly looked puzzled, which was fair enough. But she wasn't screaming. Betsy felt a little bubble of hope.

The bubble didn't have a chance to grow any bigger. Just then, the footman cleared his throat, and made another announcement.

"Miss Alice O'Golly," he declared. A very ill girl staggered into the room, and looked around blearily.

"I came," she announced thickly through a bunged-up nose. "I'm going to shing after all. I'm shorry I'm late." The effort of this speech made her sway a bit, and she leaned against the footman for support. There was a confused silence.

Sarah looked from Alice to Betsy, utterly perplexed. "But this young girl says you sent her as a replacement, with her – ah – mice," she said. Betsy's face burned, and she looked helplessly at Alexander. *Now* what?

"Excuse me," said a new voice from the audience. The hats swivelled gleefully. This was *much* better than the usual Gala concerts.

Betsy's chest tightened: she knew that voice. It was her mother.

Bella stood. "She isn't replacing

Alice. She's replacing *me*. I was supposed to be playing after Alice, but my fingers are still recovering from a temporary baking injury." She smiled proudly at Betsy. "This is my daughter."

"But," said Sarah, "I didn't ask for *her* as a replacement, I asked for—"

"Me," agreed Grandad, standing up now. "And I had to turn it down, as I'm out of practice, and didn't have any time to rehearse. As I told you. But we didn't want to let you down, so we brought Betsy."

"And the mice,"
added Bella.

"Who are here on purpose," Bertram piped up, catching on, but slightly overdoing it.

Betsy was glad no one was asking *her* any questions right now, because her brain was whirling. She had no idea Bella and Grandad had been asked to perform!

So *that* was why the family had received invitations to the Gala. And those messages on the answering machine weren't about the cake delivery at all: they were about the performance.

She remembered a pink-and-pleased Bella getting that phone call before the party, and promising to tell Betsy all about it after Bertram's big night – by which time, of course, Alexander had made his request. And Bella had believed in their bakery *so much* that instead of resting her fingers to let them heal in time, she had given up the Gala performance, without even telling them – and Grandad had turned down the performance too, to help in the kitchen instead of rehearsing.

Betsy wanted to run and hug both of them. They *had* been behind her Big Idea.

Meanwhile, Vernon was still Vernoning around at maximum volume. "This is preposterous!" he declared. "This is absurd! Mice don't play pianos!"

Betsy smiled, and cleared her throat.

"Mice," she said. "Mazurka, please."

And the mice whisked away out of sight, into the piano's belly, and began to play. The room filled with glorious twinkling music. It sounded like spring springing. It sounded like blossom blossoming. It sounded like forty-four tiny mice, who were indeed absurd, but didn't care.

Betsy watched the Queen, and waited. A sea of hats watched the Queen, and waited. Poor Alice staggered dizzily into a chair, while Sarah had a little sit-down by Prince Alphonse the Nice.

"Your Majesty," said Vernon. "I must protest—"

The Queen held up a hand. Vernon stopped. Betsy murmured "Pause" to the mice.

"One would like to know," she said quietly, "who this man is, and why he is causing a disturbance during one's Gala performance?"

"Vernon Brick, Your Majesty," said Vernon. "Chief Health and Safety Inspector for the Greater London Area. I am here to detain this mouse – er, mice. They are pests, and—"

"One," said the Queen sternly, "is enjoying their performance."

For the first time, a note of doubt crept into

Vernon's voice. "But Your Majesty, they're *mice*."

The Queen responded to this with magnificent silence, which somehow managed to convey how *very* rude it was to think that the Queen might not know a mouse when she saw one. Rude, and possibly treasonous.

Vernon ploughed on. "I am highly qualified to remove pests, Your Majesty," he said. "I have training in—"

The Queen sighed. "Then perhaps," she said, "you are highly qualified to remove yourself."

Nobody knew whether they were allowed to laugh at this. There were a lot of smothered giggles, and one very loud "HA!" from the back that was hastily cut short. Betsy had to work hard to keep her polite face in place.

"But Your Majesty," spluttered Vernon, "it is my duty to inspect—"

The Queen turned right round in her seat to look at him this time. "Quite so," she said. "But it is *not* your duty to be an insufferably gloomy killjoy. Footman, please show this man out." She turned back to face Betsy. "You may resume."

Betsy wanted to laugh; she wanted to turn and grin at Alexander and give him a huge thumbs up; she wanted to give the Queen a hug. But she sat with her hands folded politely in her lap, and very politely she said, "Mice. Mazurka."

So the mice played merrily. And the Queen and her guests sat very attentively, hats very still, and listened to the forty-four most remarkable Hazards in all of the Greater London Area.

CHAPTER TWELVE

THE HALF-MOON BAKERY AGAIN

The mice were a hit, and so were the cakes, although everyone was too busy trying to be polite and to balance their hats to *really* pay attention to their food. Betsy felt proud as she watched the cakes sail around on silver platters. But it had been more fun, in a way, when they had been wrapped in greaseproof paper and ribbon under the blossom tree.

She and the family ran to each other to hug straightaway, of course, and exchange stories.

"Mum! You never said you were meant to be playing!" said Betsy.

"Well, I was only asked just before the bakery party," said Bella, "and I didn't want to steal your father's big moment, so I saved up the news. And once I realized I would be needed in the kitchen and couldn't do both – well, then it didn't seem right to mention it."

"But it was such a big chance for you! And you too, Grandad…"

"Oh, I didn't want to do it," said Grandad. "I never play at things like this. No point. I told your mother, no one can hear you past the massive hats anyway."

"You shouldn't have given it up, either of you," said Bertram, blinking wonderingly at them. "My family are much too good to me."

"Don't be silly," said Bella. "We're a team."

Then the Queen came over to thank Betsy graciously for the performance, and thank Alexander graciously for the cakes. Betsy wasn't sure what to say to that last bit, but Alexander didn't hesitate.

"Change of plan, Your Majesty," he said. "These are not my cakes. They came from the magnificent Half-Moon Bakery – owned by Betsy's family, in fact." And he introduced the others, one by one.

"What a remarkable family," said the Queen. She looked at Betsy with the slightest smile, and suddenly Betsy was very, very sure that the Queen hadn't been fooled by her story for one second. But all she said was, "The cakes are exceptional. I would like you to bake for my next Gala. And perhaps Mrs Bow-Linnet and Mr Bow would play the piano for us next time."

The Gala was nice, but the party at the Half-Moon Bakery afterwards was nicer. It was just the Bow-Linnets and Alexander. Betsy left the mice at home, where no one could think they were a hazard. She gave them lots of extra pumpkin seeds, and checked that D-flat-to-D had stopped quivering. He had, of course. The mice never quivered for long.

At the Half-Moon they put out tea lights on one of the lemon-yellow tables, and ordered in pizza to celebrate the day's success. Then Betsy and Alexander told the others the whole story.

When Bertram discovered that Alexander was also a baker the conversation got a bit boring, while the two of them compared notes on kneading and ovens and things, and

Bertram explained at length an idea he had for transforming how vanilla custard is made. This got him very excited, and involved some complicated diagrams on napkins.

Grandad had a quick nap, but Alexander was very interested.

"I miss all this," he sighed. "I think I'll go back to my old bakery, if they'll have me."

"But what about becoming Royal Baker?" said Betsy.

Alexander shrugged. "The Royal Taster was furious when he heard I had lied to him about the cakes, so that's out of the question now. But that's OK. I don't think I was really cut out for it." He chewed a slice of pizza thoughtfully. "You know, I think I'm only middling-good at baking. I'm just really good at icing. You can distract most people if the icing is fancy enough." And he wafted his lace around elegantly, as though to demonstrate the point.

All the Bow-Linnets looked at each other, except Grandad, who snored gently.

"Alexander," said Bella, "are you telling us that you can operate a piping bag without gluing your nostrils together?"

Alexander looked confused. "How would it get in your nostrils?"

"Don't ask," said Bertram. "Listen, this bakery recently lost a chef – well, forty-four chefs to be precise. And we could use someone with your skills. Would you be interested in working here at the Half-Moon?"

And Alexander was so interested in this that he choked on the pizza, and went on spluttering for ages and ages. This woke up Grandad, who banged him enthusiastically on the back but hit his elbows on the wall again in the process, so Bella ran to get him peas, and for a minute it was chaos. Then there was a rap on the door.

Everyone stopped, and fell quiet.

It came again: *rap rap rap*. The smart rap of a walking stick. Bertram paled. He got up and opened the door as bravely as he could manage.

"Good evening," he suggested – because you could never be sure, with Great-Aunt Agatha.

The dusk was almost proper darkness outside, and Great-Aunt Agatha was a shadow against it, filling the doorway. "You have been shut all day," she announced. "I wanted cakes. Why was this bakery closed?"

Bertram drew himself up tall. "We were at a Royal Gala, Great-Aunt. They were serving our cakes."

"Why?" barked Great-Aunt Agatha. "I thought you wanted to run a bakery?"

"Yes, I—"

"Well, you can't do that *and* keep shutting everything down to work for the Palace." She gave him a rap across the knees with her stick. "Make up your mind. I'll be wanting cakes tomorrow. Goodnight, Bertram." And with that, the shadow of Great-Aunt Agatha went sailing off down the road, melting back into the dark.

Everyone looked at each other.

"Who was *that*?" said Alexander.

"Great-Aunt Agatha," said everybody else, in a miserable chorus.

"She's got a point, Dad," said Betsy. "Do you *want* to do the next Gala?"

Bertram considered this. He looked out of the doorway, and up at the moon in the sky, which had waned almost to a crescent now.

"What I would like," he said, trying out this new phrase in his mouth, "is to work on my vanilla custard idea. And I won't have time to do both. But I'm not sure it will even work – I might just be wasting time."

"Oh, but it's *interesting*," said Alexander. "I'll help. We can do it after the baking each morning."

"Do it, darling," said Bella.

"Do it, Dad," said Betsy. "Tell the Queen you're busy."

"No," said Grandad, "just tell her that Galas are a terrible waste of time."

"Right," said Bertram. He pushed his glasses up his nose. "*Right*." Then – "It's a shame the moon's waned. We ought to have a half-moon for good luck."

But they didn't need a half-moon for luck, because it didn't really matter whether the idea worked out or not. It was the right kind of Big Idea – the kind you want from the inside out – the kind that made Bertram push his glasses up importantly, and Alexander roll up his lacy sleeves. It made the night feel alive with possibility.

"We'll be OK without the luck, I reckon," said Betsy. And she was right, of course.

ABOUT THE AUTHOR

Sylvia Bishop spent an entire childhood reading
fiction, dreaming up stories and pretending.
Now she writes her stories down for a living,
preferably by lamp-light with tea. Her first book,
Erica's Elephant, was published in 2016. She has
since written two further titles for young readers,
The Bookshop Girl and *A Sea of Stories*, and two
middle-grade mysteries, *The Secret of the Night
Train* and *Trouble in New York*. Her books
have been translated into sixteen languages,
including French, Dutch, Russian and Japanese.
Find out more at sylviabishopbooks.com.

ABOUT THE ILLUSTRATOR

Ashley King is an illustrator working in leafy Warwickshire. He has a bachelor's degree with honors in Illustration and Animation. He skillfully hand draws all his creations with humour and emotion mixed with a digital twist. Ashley is the illustrator of many children's books, including the *Witch for a Week* series by Kaye Umansky and *The Magical Adventures of Whoops the Wonder Dog* by TV chef Glynn Purnell. This will be the fifth book Ashley has illustrated for Sylvia.

Read about Betsy's other adventures...

When Betsy receives a mysterious letter offering a Method to make her piano playing 'stupendous', she jumps at the chance. There's just one small condition: Betsy must keep the Method a secret.

When a circus comes to town, Betsy slips away to see the show. But so too do her forty-four mice! As chaos ensues, Betsy finds herself facing up to the odious ringmaster, Chester Fry...